p6

The Cold Cash Caper

When Frank reached the parking lot, only a few cars remained. Relieved to see that the minivan was one of them, he turned and headed back toward the bridge. But as he drew near, Frank's stomach clenched. His brother was struggling with two men wearing ski masks in the middle of the bridge.

Joe's hand shot out and delivered a karate chop to the taller man's throat. The shorter man wrapped his arms around Joe from behind.

Frank rushed to Joe's aid, taking down the shorter man with a flying tackle. As Frank scrambled to his feet, he saw Joe hit the taller man in the solar plexus. The man bent double as the air rushed from his lungs.

Just when it looked as if the boys were going to hold their own, the shorter man lunged at Joe. His weight slammed Joe into the railing of the bridge. With a loud snap, the old wood splintered.

Joe appeared to hang in midair for a moment. Then, with an ear-splitting scream, he dropped from sight. . . .

The Hardy Boys Mystery Stories

Available from MINSTREL Books

THE HARDY BOYS®

136

THE COLD CASH CAPER

FRANKLIN W. DIXON

A MINSTREL® BOOK

Published by POCKET BOOKS
New York London Toronto Sydney Tokyo Singapore

This book is a work of fiction. Names, characters, places and incidents are products of the author's imagination or are used fictitiously. Any resemblance to actual events or locales or persons, living or dead, is entirely coincidental.

A MINSTREL PAPERBACK *Original*

 A Minstrel Book published by
POCKET BOOKS, a division of Simon & Schuster Inc.
1230 Avenue of the Americas, New York, NY 10020

Copyright © 1996 by Simon & Schuster Inc.

Produced by Mega-Books, Inc.

ISBN: 0-671-50520-3

First Minstrel Books printing April 1996

10 9 8 7 6 5 4 3 2 1

THE HARDY BOYS MYSTERY STORIES is a trademark of Simon & Schuster Inc.

THE HARDY BOYS, A MINSTREL BOOK and colophon are registered trademarks of Simon & Schuster Inc.

Printed in the U.S.A.

Contents

THE COLD
CASH CAPER

1 Wipeout

"All right!" Joe Hardy cheered as he climbed behind the wheel of his van. "A three-day weekend! There's snow on the ground, the winter festival is starting, and there's no school until next Tuesday. Is this for real?"

Frank Hardy, who at eighteen was a year older than Joe, brushed the snowflakes out of his dark hair. He shivered as he glanced through the windshield at the thick layer of clouds up in the sky.

"What's up, Frank?" Joe asked his brother. "You seem kind of bummed."

"Not bummed—just frozen solid. Crank up that heater, will you?" Frank said. "Doesn't February feel like the longest month of the year?"

"That's just your imagination," Joe said with a

1

laugh. "You'll forget all about the weather by tonight when the winter festival starts," he said, backing out of the parking space. "I can't wait to get out on the ice."

Frank grinned. "You won't be saying that when you see me fly past you on the race course."

"Good luck, bro. We both know I'm the speed-skating champion around here. Hey," Joe said, changing the subject as he pulled out of the school's parking lot. "Why do you think Dad called school and told us to come straight home?"

"Who knows?" Frank said with a shrug. "But it must be important. Maybe he wanted to give us last-minute instructions before he leaves for his crime seminar in New York."

Frank was proud of the name their father had made for himself as a private detective. Frank and Joe had learned a lot from their dad and put it to good use solving some of Bayport's most puzzling crimes.

"When Dad was talking about the newest methods of DNA testing last night, I almost wished I was going with him," Frank added. "We should be up on the latest techniques."

Joe stopped at a red light. "What? And miss all the fun at the winter festival?"

"I said *almost*. No way I'd miss the cross-country skiing event," Frank said. "I have to beat you at something!"

Since they were so close in age, Frank and Joe

always had a friendly competition going. Where Joe was blond-haired and quite muscular, Frank had dark hair and a slighter build, though he was an inch taller. Each one had his special talents, and when it came to solving mysteries, they worked together as a team.

The snowfall had thickened considerably by the time Joe pulled into the driveway in front of the Hardy home. An intense aroma of baking cookies greeted them as they hurried into the house.

"We're back here, boys," Laura Hardy, their mother, called.

In the kitchen, Gertrude Hardy, their father's sister, was pulling a pan of cookies from the oven. Her expression was worried and upset as she looked at the baking sheet.

"What's the matter, Aunt Gertrude?" Joe asked. "Did something go wrong with your world-famous chocolate-chip cookie recipe?"

"Heavens no," Aunt Gertrude said with a laugh. "Leona Turner loves them so much, she insisted I bake another five dozen."

Frank glanced at the mound of boxes and tins that other volunteers had dropped off. "Looks to me like you've already got enough cookies to feed all of Bayport."

"My point exactly," Aunt Gertrude said. "If Leona Turner runs her gift shop the way she does the booths, it's no wonder she's broke all the time. She does tend to get a little carried away."

3

Joe reached for a cookie, while Frank poured them both glasses of milk. Frank was just taking a big bite out of a cookie when his father, Fenton Hardy, walked into the kitchen. There was a smile tugging at the corners of his mouth. All at once, both Frank and Joe started asking him why he'd called them at school.

"One at a time," Fenton said, holding his hands up. "I've got some news I think you'll like. Ron Smithson, the festival director, called me. It seems that David Kennedy, the figure-skating star they booked for the closing ceremonies, is tired of the media poking microphones in his face. He wants to be with kids his own age for a change. Smithson wants you to act as Kennedy's escort while he's in town—pick him up at the airport and show him the sights."

"David Kennedy wants us to hang out with him?" Frank said in disbelief. "The winter festival just got about ten times more exciting."

"No kidding," Joe agreed. "Do you remember how he came from behind to win the gold medal in the last Olympics? His trademark triple axel is truly awesome."

"Let's just hope he doesn't throw a tantrum while he's here," Frank added, remembering that Kennedy was also known for his bad behavior. "Didn't he trash his hotel room in London a while back?"

"He's pulled some crazy stunts," Fenton said.

4

"Once he failed to show up for a performance. He had to find himself a new coach after that."

"He also loves to argue with the judges at competitions," Frank added. "And I've heard sometimes he refuses to give out autographs."

Joe shoved down another cookie. "Who cares about his manners?" he said, his mouth full. "It's going to be incredible just to hang out with the guy."

"I'm glad you're excited," Fenton said with a smile. "His plane arrives tomorrow morning at ten o'clock."

Laura Hardy reminded her husband that their train to New York was due to leave in a half hour. Fenton and Laura were heading out the front of the house just as Frank and Joe's friend Chet Morton walked in through the back door.

"Bet you can't guess who's gonna be riding on the lead float in the festival parade," Chet announced, red-faced and excited.

Joe grinned. "And I bet you're going to tell us anyway."

"Check it out!" Chet turned sideways and held a hand above his eyes, as if trying to see through a thick fog. "That's Washington crossing the Delaware, just in case you guys flunked history."

"We got it," Frank said. "We got it."

Chet dropped the pose and sniffed the air. "Sure does smell good in here."

"Cookies are on the table. Help yourself,

5

George," Aunt Gertrude said with a smile. Then she took off her apron, straightened her suit, and turned to the boys. "I'm late for the committee meeting. Would you mind dropping off these cookies and cupcakes at the recreation center when you get to the park?"

"No problem," Frank said.

Frank and Joe were going over to the festival to practice speed skating. Chet agreed to come along, and all three boys loaded the van with Aunt Gertrude's cookies.

Climbing into the back of the van, Chet said, "I'll make sure none of these boxes slide around too much."

As Frank pulled away, Chet gulped down the last of his cookies and lifted the lid of the nearest box. "Wow! Chocolate cupcakes. What else is in here?"

Frank turned to Joe. "Maybe you should trade places with Chet."

"Good idea," Joe teased. "We wouldn't want to deliver a bunch of empty boxes."

"Very funny," Chet said grumpily. Because he was big, everyone liked to kid Chet about his appetite. "Can I help it if your aunt makes the best cookies this side of the Mississippi? Hey! I almost forgot. Have you seen the festival brochure? They added something new this year—a tubing hill. You know, you sit in the middle of a big truck inner tube and slide down the hill. I can't wait to try it out."

"Sounds like fun," Frank said.

"Hanging out with David Kennedy is the best thing about this whole festival," Joe said.

"You mean David Kennedy the skater? The Olympic athlete?" Chet asked excitedly.

"You got it," Joe said, and explained to Chet what he and Frank had been assigned.

"Incredible," Chet said. "I'm going to add his autograph to my collection."

"Whoa, Chet. Time out," Frank said. "The reason we've been assigned the job of escorting Kennedy is because he's tired of being mauled by the media and by fans."

"Yeah," Joe added. "Try to be cool around him. Treat him just like any other kid. That's what he wants and what we're going to deliver."

"Okay," Chet said. "No problem."

Only a few large flakes were still falling by the time Frank stopped for a red light at the corner of the park. The cross street, Park Avenue, was closed to traffic for the festival. Huge blocks of ice lined the sidewalk, ready for the ice-sculpting contest. Booths featuring crafts and hot food and drinks were already set up in the street. Even though the festival games hadn't started yet, the booths were doing a brisk business with people coming to check out the fairgrounds. The light turned green, and Frank drove along the edge of the park. On his left was the city auditorium. Just before the road curved sharply to the left, Frank turned right into the parking lot.

"Too bad someone didn't decorate that." Chet pointed to the dilapidated Bradford mansion, hovering like a vulture on top of Bayport's tallest hill. "It gives me the creeps."

The estate's sizable yard, neglected for years, sloped down to abut the edge of the park. Paint peeled from the sagging three-story house, and gnarled shrubbery grew twenty feet high. The twenty-acre estate had been deserted since Old Man Bradford died.

There was still about an hour of daylight left for the boys to get in some practice on the ice. They jumped out of the van, loaded their arms with boxes and tins, and headed to the recreation center. Along the way, Frank saw people busy stringing gold lights in the trees and hanging brightly colored banners from the lampposts. From the stables, he could hear the sounds of sleigh bells and neighing horses.

The recreation center was an old indoor skating rink, located on a slight hill next to the lake. Many of the festival booths were located inside the building. The boys carried the boxes inside and delivered them to a booth where Aunt Gertrude's coworkers were busy setting out cakes and cookies. After saying a quick hello, Frank, Joe, and Chet went back to the van for a second load.

When they reached their van, a car pulled into the slot next to them. Joe was busy gathering boxes and tins and didn't pay any attention until a sneering voice sliced through the wintry chill.

"Well, well, if it isn't Joe Hardy, the hotshot hockey player from Bayport High."

Joe spun around so fast he almost dropped the boxes in his hands. "Oh, it's you, Thompson. I should have known."

Craig Thompson was a little shorter than Joe and husky like Chet. Thompson was eighteen, Frank's age, and goalie for Bayport's rival, Cross Town High. Less than a week earlier, Joe had racked up a hat trick against him, scoring three goals and winning the championship game for Bayport. Thompson was furious at the time, and he vowed to Joe he'd get even.

As Thompson tied the laces of his skates together and hung them over his shoulder, he gritted his teeth so hard a muscle twitched in his square jaw. "I hope you entered the speed sprint, Hardy. Everyone will see what a phony you are when I come in first instead of you."

Frank held his breath, waiting for Joe to react. Joe could be a real hothead if he wasn't careful. But this time, Joe simply glared back at the boy.

"Go for it, Thompson," Joe said coolly. "Just

don't blame me when you lose again." Then Joe turned around, used his foot to close the van door, and started marching toward the bridge.

Frank and Chet caught up with him inside the park. The boys entered the rec hall and dropped the boxes and tins off at the booth, then went outside and headed toward the lake.

"Nice going," Frank said to his brother. "You didn't let that creep get to you."

"What's the point?" Joe said. "Why give the guy the satisfaction of seeing me blow my cool?" Suddenly Joe slapped his hand to his head. "I forgot my skates! They're in the van. You guys go ahead—I'll meet up with you on the ice."

Frank and Chet headed over to the rink where the speed skating would take place. Craig Thompson was already on the ice, along with a couple of his buddies. Workers busily lined the wooden wall surrounding the rink with protective bales of hay.

Joe arrived back at the rink a few moments later. He quickly laced up his skates and took to the ice. Frank watched as Joe glided around the rink to warm up. Soon Joe was bent over, resting his left arm on his back in the classic racing stance. He gradually picked up his pace, his newly sharpened blades cutting a clean line in the ice.

The wind whipped through Joe's blond hair as he blew by Frank. Joe took the next curve at racing speed. His thighs poured on the steam, and his swinging arms added momentum to his stride.

Frank held his breath. Joe was going so fast that one mistake meant he'd crash.

As Joe went into the curve, his form was perfect. The razor-thin edges on his skates held the turn tight. One foot crossed in front of the other, the rhythm sure and steady.

"Way to go!" Frank shouted from the side.

"Go for it!" Chet joined in.

Joe was just coming out of the turn when suddenly he stumbled. Frank watched in horror as Joe tripped over his feet and started frantically waving his arms to keep his balance.

There was a sharp metallic clang. Joe pitched forward and started to fall. Frank realized with a shock what had happened: the blade on Joe's left skate had snapped right off.

2 Finger of Suspicion

Joe Hardy hit the ice with a bone-jarring, teeth-rattling crunch. Like a hockey puck, he began sliding at breakneck speed toward the wall.

Two workers dropped a hay bale and jumped out of his way. Now there was nothing but the bale between Joe and the wall. Joe slammed into the hay so fast it barely slowed him down. He tumbled over and over. A moment later he went flying sideways into the wall.

"Yeooww!" Joe cried, making contact with an ear-splitting cry.

Next to him, the wall shuddered and creaked, and then a section split in two. Joe held his hands over his head, protecting himself from the splintering wood.

Frank raced toward him, straight across the ice. He came skidding to a stop at his brother's feet.

"Are you all right? Is anything broken?" Frank asked.

Tentatively, Joe moved an arm, then a leg. "I don't think so. Just bruised."

Frank pulled Joe to his feet. "What happened? I saw your blade fly off. Didn't you just have those skates tuned and sharpened for the races?"

Joe held his foot up to examine the dangling blade. "Tell me about it," he said, and headed off the ice, skating on his right foot, pushing off with the left.

The group of onlookers opened a path, and Joe limped toward the bench. He noticed that Craig Thompson snickered as Joe passed him.

"Yeah, right," Joe said under his breath. "We'll see who has the last laugh."

The onlookers, realizing that Joe was okay, all began drifting away. Chet rushed to his friend's side and asked, "Are you all right? I thought you were a goner!"

"I'm fine, but I'm not sure about my skate," Joe said. He began unlacing his skates, eager to take a closer look. Joe already had an idea that his blade flying off was anything but an accident. He put on his boots, then picked up the broken skate. A second later his suspicions were confirmed.

"Check it out," Joe said. "The back screws on

13

my blade are missing, and the front two are about to fall out."

"That doesn't make sense," Frank said, taking a closer look. "They always tighten the screws at the shop when they sharpen the blades."

"Exactly," Joe confirmed. "Besides, I checked them before I left the house, and the blades were tight. My guess is someone loosened them on purpose, just enough so they'd work free after I'd been on the ice awhile."

"Who would do something that crazy?" Chet asked.

Joe looked over to where Craig Thompson and his buddies were laughing. They seemed to be enjoying their own private joke. "I have a pretty good idea," Joe said. "When I went back to get my skates, the van was unlocked. I must have forgotten to lock the door when I had that run-in with Thompson."

"And he was still there when we left the parking lot," Frank pointed out.

Joe kicked at the snow with his shoe. "Thompson must have known he'd get away with it, too. I can't say anything if I don't have proof."

"True," Frank agreed. "But think of it this way: when you beat him in the speed sprint, you'll have all the proof that matters. Proof that you're the fastest, that is."

"True enough," Joe said. "But if I'm really going to be fast, I'd better get this blade fixed. I've

14

got some extra screws in my skating bag in the van." Joe checked his watch. "We have some time before the opening ceremonies. Want to come with me?"

"Sure," Frank said. "There's nothing happening here."

"Chet?" Joe asked.

"I think I'll check out the tubing hill," Chet said. "I'll meet you at the rec hall later."

A crowd was already gathering for the opening ceremonies. The Hardys fought their way through the incoming crowd as they headed past the recreation center and down the hill toward the parking lot. Joe unlocked the van and climbed in. Frank turned on the overhead map light as Joe rummaged through his skating bag. Within a few minutes, Joe had fixed his blade with a screwdriver from the toolbox they carried for emergencies.

"That should do it," Joe said, checking that the blade was tight.

"You can test it out after the ceremonies are over," Frank said.

"Good idea," Joe said. He tied his laces together and hung his skates over his shoulder. "It's nearly dark. Let's go find Chet."

Joe locked the van, and he and Frank started toward the park entrance. Excitement hung in the air as they hurried along the path. When they reached the rec hall, Joe scanned the thinning crowd, looking for Chet. Booths lined the walls of the huge room. Joe quickly spotted Chet at one of the tables in the middle of the room.

Chet waved them over. "About time," he called out. "Everyone else is already out by the lake for the opening ceremony."

It took a few minutes, but eventually Frank, Joe, and Chet managed to work their way to the front of the crowd. The men and women who ran the festival sat facing the onlookers in a semicircle of chairs set up on a small platform.

"Whew, just made it," Joe said.

There was a series of loud noises, and fireworks began to light up the sky over the lake. Joe looked at his watch. "Six o'clock. Right on time."

A few minutes later the fireworks ended, and Ira Meffert, head of the Bayport Children's Hospital, rose from his chair and stepped up to the microphone.

"Thirty years ago Louis R. Bradford discovered that the Bayport Children's Hospital didn't have enough money to continue to operate. He suggested raising funds by holding a winter festival. It took a lot of hard work by a lot of dedicated volunteers, but they did it . . . and have been doing it every year since then."

The crowd broke into cheers and applause. Meffert smiled and held up his hands for silence.

"I want to thank three people who have worked especially hard, beginning with Leona Turner. She has the task of overseeing all the booths,"

16

Meffert said. "So when you're enjoying a cup of cider or admiring your new hand-knitted sweater, thank her." After polite applause, Meffert leaned toward the microphone. "Roger Pender moved to our town only recently, but he has worked tirelessly on behalf of the festival. Not only is he chairman of the parade committee, he actually talked Jack Wilson into donating a brand-new car for the raffle."

A tall young man, around twenty-eight or so, with dark hair and slim build, stepped forward as the crowd broke into more applause.

"And last but certainly not least," Meffert said, "I give you Ron Smithson, the festival director and the man responsible for putting it all together. Thanks, everyone! And have a great time."

The crowd gave a last round of applause. Joe opened his program to see what was scheduled for that evening. "Hey, guys, check this out. It says here that the winner in the speed-skating sprint gets a gift certificate from Hi-Tech Outlet. I could get that new video game I've been wanting."

"Don't count on it," came a voice from Joe's left.

Joe looked up. Craig Thompson had stopped a few feet away and stood glaring at him.

"I guess we'll see, won't we," Joe said. Then he turned to the others. "Come on, guys. Let's head over to the lake."

"You want to try out those skates?" Frank asked.

"Maybe," Joe replied. "Or maybe I don't like the company around here."

Thompson shot Joe a mean look as the group moved off, but Joe refused to glance back. If he was right, and Thompson was low enough to have sabotaged his skates, he didn't owe the guy a polite goodbye.

At the lake, music drifted from loudspeakers. The ice had quickly filled with skaters from the crowd. Nearby small children piled into horse-drawn sleighs for rides around the park.

"How about getting some roasted chestnuts?" Chet suggested.

"Are you hungry again?" Joe asked.

"Those cookies were hours ago," Chet insisted.

"Go on ahead, Chet," Frank said. "I think I'll skate with Joe for a while. We'll hook up with you later."

After a good twenty minutes on the ice, Joe felt reassured that his blade was going to hold this time. By then he and Frank were hungry, and they decided to find Chet and maybe pick up some of their aunt Gertrude's cookies.

The rec hall was packed with festival goers. The boys were working their way through the crowd, looking for Chet, when the sound of raised voices caught their attention. Curious, they approached a circle of angry people. Chet stood in the center of the group. A very capable-looking security guard in his early thirties, dressed in a khaki uniform, had a firm grip on his arm. Chet's face was red, and he looked flustered.

"I don't know what you're talking about," Chet said to the guard.

"Don't play dumb," a second security guard said, grabbing Chet by the arm. "Is he the one or not?" he asked the other uniformed man.

"That's him," the tall, thin security guard confirmed. He shook an accusing finger in Chet's face. "He's the guy who stole the money!"

3 A Warning

"I don't know what you're talking ab-b-bout," Chet stammered. "I'm telling you—you've got the wrong guy!"

"Then explain *that*," the thin security guard said, pointing to a white ski mask in Chet's hand. "That's what the thief used to disguise himself."

"I swear I've never seen this ski mask before in my life," Chet insisted.

Joe didn't know why Chet was holding the ski mask, but he did know that Chet wouldn't steal a pack of gum, much less take money from the children's hospital funds. He nudged Frank. "Come on. We've got to do something."

The Hardys pushed their way to the center of the irate group. Officer Con Riley was there, along with Ira Meffert, Roger Pender, Leona Turner, and Ron Smithson. Con had helped out the Hardys on a case more than once. Joe was counting on the man to look after a friend of theirs, too.

"Officer Riley, you know that Chet is our friend," Joe said. "Do you mind telling us what's going on?"

"That's what I'm trying to find out," Con Riley said, sounding frustrated. He turned to the thin security guard. "Okay, Adams. Tell me exactly what happened."

"I picked up the money bags from the booths over on Park Avenue the way Mr. Meyers here told me and was on my way to deliver them. Then this guy"—Josh Adams jerked a thumb toward Chet—"stepped out from behind a tree and shoved a gun in my face. He was wearing that ski mask."

"If the thief was wearing a mask, how did you see his face?" Joe asked.

"I didn't, but that's him all right," Adams said. "The thief had on a maroon jacket and was five ten or so, and burly."

Joe noted with a sinking feeling that Chet was wearing a maroon jacket and fit the guard's physical description perfectly.

"And there was a blue bolt of lightning on the side of that ski mask."

Joe watched as Chet turned the ski mask over, looked at the lightning bolt, and gulped. "But I'm telling you, I didn't do it," Chet said.

21

"So how'd you get the mask?" the guard holding on to Chet's arm asked with a sneer. His badge indicated that he was head of security, and that his name was Dan Meyers.

"I found it by the side of the path," Chet told Meyers, swallowing hard. "I brought it here to turn in to the lost-and-found."

"Likely story," someone in the crowd said.

"I'll take charge of that. It's evidence," Officer Riley said. Chet handed him the ski mask.

Dan Meyers kept a firm grip on Chet's arm. "Okay, son. Why don't you tell us what you did with the money?"

"I didn't take it. You've got to believe me," Chet said. Then, with a look of desperation, he turned to Frank and Joe. "You guys have to help me. Do something. Clear my name."

"Where did the robbery take place?" Frank asked.

"I came in through the Park Avenue entrance and was rounding the lake," Adams said. "Happened just after I passed the path to the picnic area."

"What time was that?" Officer Riley asked.

"Around six. Mr. Meffert was just about to give his speech," Adams answered.

"Then Chet couldn't have been the thief," Joe said, remembering that he looked at his watch just as the fireworks began and right before Meffert made his speech.

"That's right," Frank agreed. "He was with us. We were all at the lake. Besides, you said the robber was armed. When you searched Chet, did you find a gun?"

"Meyers?" Officer Riley asked.

Dan Meyers's face dropped in resignation. "No," he admitted. "He didn't have a gun."

"Looks like we've got the wrong man," Officer Riley said. "Turn him loose, Meyers."

The crowd murmured and began to disperse now that the excitement was over. Joe turned to Officer Riley. "Frank and I could check the park for someone matching Chet's description."

"Hold on a second," Meyers piped in. "That job calls for someone with experience, not boys."

"These boys are experienced detectives," Ron Smithson, the festival director, said. "And they know the people and the area. It might not be a bad idea if Frank and Joe help out with this case." Smithson turned to the Hardys. "In fact, I'm all for it."

Joe smiled at his brother and Chet. "Thanks, Mr. Smithson," he said. "We won't let you down."

Meyers let out a long sigh, which Smithson chose to ignore. Instead, the festival director said, "Good. Report directly to Meyers. Dan, give these boys all the help you can. We need to get that money back!"

Meyers's face went red. He turned to stalk off, but Con Riley called out his name and the man turned around. "You'll have to fill out a police report," said Riley. "I'll bring it down to your office right away. And make sure Adams is there to give a statement."

"Right," Meyers said, and walked away.

The Hardys and Chet watched him go, then Frank turned to Smithson and said, "We'll get to work right away."

Smithson gave the three boys a confident nod, then went off toward the festival offices at the back of the rec hall. Leona Turner, Roger Pender, and Mr. Meffert left with him.

"It's still only seven-thirty," Joe said after the group had gone. "There's a chance the thief thinks he got away with his stunt and is still hanging around. Why don't we look around for someone answering Chet's description?"

"Good idea. We can cover more ground if we split up," Frank said. "I'll take the Park Avenue entrance. Joe, take the parking lot. Chet, check around the lake."

Chet shook his head vehemently. He still had a scared look in his eyes. "No way," he said. "I'm sticking close to one of you guys. If something else happens, I want to be sure I've got an alibi."

"Fair enough," Frank said with a laugh. "Okay. Why don't you guys start with the crowd at the lake? If we're lucky, maybe someone will remember seeing a suspicious guy in a hurry."

"Right. Let's go, Chet," Joe said.

"Meet me at the van in an hour," Frank called over his shoulder.

Joe and Chet didn't have much luck spotting a likely suspect around the lake. After a half hour of searching, Joe suggested they ask around the parking lot to see if anyone had noticed someone acting suspicious. The boys left the lake, passed the rec hall, and started along the footpath toward the lot.

As they neared the old wooden bridge, Chet let out a long sigh. "This has got to be the worst day of my life," he said.

"Even with Aunt Gertrude's cookies?" Joe said. "You can't be serious!"

Chet punched Joe lightly on the arm. "I am serious. I could be in real trouble."

"Listen," Joe said, dropping his smile. "As soon as we catch the thief everything will be fine."

"Yeah, right," Chet said in a forlorn voice. "We don't even have a real clue."

Joe knew that Chet was right. The fact that the thief was built like Chet and wore a maroon jacket wasn't much to go on. A lot of guys fit that description.

In the parking lot a few festival goers ambled toward their cars. "Let's start with them," Joe said, pointing to a group gathered at the far end of the lot. "Maybe one of them saw something." Joe walked up to an old man in the group and said,

"We're investigating the robbery that happened today. Can you remember seeing someone suspicious hanging out?"

Several people in the group shook their heads. "Wish I could help, but I didn't see anyone," the old man said.

"Neither did I," a woman said.

"Thanks, anyway," Joe said, trying not to sound too dejected. After asking a few more people the same questions, Joe said to Chet, "Want to wait in the van for Frank to show up?"

"I guess," Chet said gloomily.

"What's wrong?" Joe asked as he and Chet started walking toward the van.

"What if we never prove I'm innocent?" Chet asked.

"We will—" Joe nearly slipped on the frozen ground. His right foot hit something slick and skidded off to the side. He waved his arms and regained his balance. "Must have hit a patch of ice."

"No, it's something else," Chet said, and bent over. He cleared the snow away with his hands, revealing an oblong plastic zipper bag, the kind businesses used to carry money to the bank. As he reached for it, Joe grabbed his arm.

"That could be evidence," Joe said, his excitement rising. "Don't touch it. Come on! We should take it to Officer Riley, right away."

Joe raced to the van, got a pair of pliers, came

back, and picked up the bag by the zipper tab. With a firm grip on the pliers, he shook the bag back and forth a few times. "I think there's something in here, but it doesn't feel like a lot of money. Definitely no coins," Joe said. "Well, we'll find out soon enough, I hope. Let's go!"

Joe and Chet headed back across the bridge and went straight to the rec hall. Officer Riley wasn't there, so Joe gave the bag to Meyers and explained where they found it.

"Good work," Meyers said, examining the bag. "I guess you kids are okay after all. I'll call Riley right away."

Outside, Chet didn't look quite nearly so downcast. "That's a real break, huh?" he said to Joe excitedly. "Maybe the bag has prints on it. Will they be able to find the guy?"

"One thing at a time," Joe said, holding up his hands. "We still don't even know if the money bag came from the robbery."

"Here comes Frank," Chet said, pointing to the footpath. "Let's tell him!"

"Tell me what?" Frank asked.

Joe filled Frank in, and his eyes lit up. He pounded Chet on the back and said, "Sounds like you're going to stay a free man. How does it feel?"

Chet let out a huge sigh of relief. "Like I could eat a whole pizza. Who's ready for dinner?"

"Now, that's the Chet we know," Joe said. "I'm ready. Frank?"

"Me, too," Frank said.

The crowds had thinned, and it didn't take the boys long to reach the nearly empty parking lot and pile into the van. Along the way, Frank told Joe that he'd seen Leona Turner and Roger Pender walking back to Park Avenue.

"They both own shops along the street," said Frank. "That puts them within pretty close range to the robbery."

"You don't think they're suspects, do you?" Chet asked. "They're both working hard to make the festival a success. Why ruin it with a robbery?"

"Good point," Frank said, backing the van out of its slot in the parking lot. "I'm not saying they are suspects, but we should think about who had the opportunity to rob Adams."

"And also who knew he'd be carrying cash," Joe added.

"Exactly," Frank said.

Frank exited the parking lot. As he neared the road, he slowed down and craned his neck, trying to see beyond the Bradford estate's overgrown shrubbery at the bottom of the hill.

"How's the road your way?" Frank asked his brother.

"Can't see a thing," Joe said. "The city should cut that shrubbery down. It's a traffic hazard."

The road to Frank's left was clear. "Let me

28

know if you see a car coming," he said, and continued to ease forward.

"Watch out!" Joe suddenly shouted.

Thinking a car was coming, Frank instinctively jerked the wheel to the left and slammed on the brakes. He glanced toward the right, expecting to see headlights.

Joe's eyes widened at the sight of a huge rock, the size of a grapefruit, sailing through the air. He could see it tumbling end over end as it started its downward arc.

It hit the top of the van with a loud crunch, missing the windshield by a whisker.

Joe jumped out of the van and picked up the rock, which had rolled to the ground. There was a piece of paper tied to it. He opened it and looked at the crude black letters of the note:

GET OFF THE CASE, HARDYS—OR ELSE

4 Deadly Missiles

Joe turned his gaze toward the overgrown shrubbery. Just then he caught a shadowy glimpse of a guy running through the hedge. "Hey, you!" Joe shouted, but the guy continued to flail his way through the brush.

"I'll be right back," Joe called to his brother. Then he pushed his way through the hedge to find himself standing on a driveway. On his right, a huge wrought-iron gate was set in the stone wall surrounding the Bradford estate. A padlock held a heavy chain in place. To Joe's left, the driveway descended to the road.

"Whoever threw that rock couldn't have made it up the hill already," Joe said under his breath.

That meant he must have headed toward the road. Joe ran down the driveway. He rounded some shrubbery just in time to hear a car engine start. The car pulled away before Joe could get a glimpse of the driver.

Joe kicked the ground in frustration as the car's taillights disappeared around the curve. Disappointed, he walked back up the driveway. Frank and Chet were waiting for him near the hedge.

"From the looks of this note," Frank said to Joe, "my guess is the thief has been hanging around all this time. How else would he know we're on the case?"

"True," Joe agreed. "But if he wants us off the case so badly, why would he draw attention to himself by throwing the rock? I only missed catching him by about ten seconds."

"Good question," Chet said. "He could have just left us the note under our wiper."

"Except that would have lessened the impact," Joe put in.

"Ha ha," Chet said. "Listen, guys, it's been real fun, but do you think you could drive me home now?"

"I thought you wanted pizza," Joe said.

"I did, but that was before you got your fan mail," Chet said. "Now I just want to go home, where I know I'm safe from any meteorite showers that might come my way."

Frank and Joe dropped Chet off at his home, and the boys arrived at their house shortly after. When they walked in the back door, Aunt Gertrude was sitting at the kitchen table eating take-out Chinese food.

"It's in the oven, keeping warm," she said, catching a glimpse of their hungry expressions. "I thought you would never make it home. It's almost eight-thirty!"

"We got held up at the festival," Frank said, deciding it would be better not to tell her about the rock-throwing incident.

But Aunt Gertrude was one step ahead of them. While Frank and Joe helped themselves to some food, Aunt Gertrude poured them sodas. "I heard about the robbery," she said. "I can't believe people would say such a thing about Chet."

"Luckily, Chet was with us at the time," Joe said. "Otherwise, he might be in big trouble right now."

Between bites, Frank told their aunt what he knew about the robbery, finishing with the information that Joe and Chet had found a bag that might have contained the missing money.

Gertrude's eyes went wide. "Even though the festival hadn't officially started, the booths on Park Avenue had a good day with people coming to look at the preparations. Plus, a lot of raffle tickets were sold. My guess is whoever stole the money made off with more than two thousand dollars." Aunt Gertrude sighed. "Luckily, we've got David Kennedy appearing at the closing ceremonies. Even with the robbery, the festival should still raise enough money for Bradford's trust to continue to support the hospital."

Frank swallowed, and said, "Explain to me how the Bradford trust works," he said.

"Louis Bradford worked hard for his money," Aunt Gertrude said. "He was willing to support the hospital but felt the town should do its part as well. As long as the festival raises fifty thousand dollars each year, the Bradford trust will pick up the rest of the tab. Sometimes that runs into the millions."

"What happens if the festival doesn't raise the fifty thousand?" Joe asked.

"All of Bradford's millions go to his heirs, whoever they are. Bradford had only one relative anyone knows anything about, a daughter named Dolores. She had a fight with her father years ago and left town. No one has heard from her since."

"And if they can't find this Dolores woman?" Joe asked.

"The state gets the money," Aunt Gertrude explained. She smiled and stood up from the table. "I'm sure they wouldn't mind that one bit! But what would happen to the hospital then? Think of all those children."

Frank put a reassuring hand on his aunt's arm. "Don't worry," he said. "Aren't you the one who's always saying not to cry over unspilt milk?"

Gertrude looked puzzled. "Frank, you'll have to explain yourself a bit better."

33

"One," Frank said, "we're going to solve the mystery and get the money back. Two, Bradford's millions aren't going anywhere they don't belong. And three, it's late, I'm beat, and we've got to pick up David Kennedy at the airport first thing tomorrow morning."

"In other words?" Aunt Gertrude asked with a smile.

"In other words," Joe said, rising from the table, "you're worrying over nothing." With that, he kissed his aunt good night.

Overnight an ice storm coated the power lines and tree branches with glittering icicles. As Joe opened his eyes, he caught himself blinking against the bright winter sun. He jumped out of bed, raced into Frank's room, and pushed his brother to the window. Frank's eyes widened at the sight of the icicles. "Just in time for the cross-country skiing event this afternoon. The runs should be nice and slick."

Downstairs, Aunt Gertrude had sausages, scrambled eggs, and toast on the table. After a quick breakfast, Frank and Joe stood up, ready to head off to the airport to pick up David Kennedy.

"Oh, I nearly forgot," Aunt Gertrude said. "Dan Meyers called this morning. He said to tell you the bag you found had nothing in it. Just a few empty envelopes. There weren't any prints, but he'd like you to stop by his office."

34

Joe checked his watch. "We've got time before we head on out to the airport. Frank?"

"Good idea," Frank said.

Joe was excited as Frank loaded his skis into the van. They were on a case, they had an important visitor to look after, and the festival was heading into high gear. What more could he ask for? "Should we stop by to pick up Chet?" Joe asked his brother as he started the car. "He's dying to meet David Kennedy."

"He called just before I left the house," Frank told Joe. "He says he's too down to come to the festival today."

"Wow, that's not like Chet," Joe said.

"I know," Frank said, nodding. "But I have a feeling that until we catch the real thief, Chet isn't going to be his usual chipper self. He thinks everyone will be pointing fingers at him and calling him a thief."

The roads were icy, so Joe took it easy. When they reached the park, the brightly colored banners, the sounds of laughter and sleigh bells gave it a festive air. After Joe found a parking place, he and Frank hurried toward the rec hall. The boys crossed the huge expanse of wooden floor to a door at the back. It opened into a narrow hall where the festival committee had its offices. The door to the security office stood open.

When Joe knocked, Dan Meyers looked up. "Come in. Have a seat, boys," he said. For a long moment, Meyers studied them thoughtfully. Then he smiled to reveal a row of crooked teeth. "Finding that bag was good work," he said finally.

"Thanks," Frank said. "Too bad there weren't any prints on it."

"If we coordinate our efforts, we should be able to wrap this case up in no time," Meyers said.

Meyers opened a desk drawer and pulled out two badges and handed them to the boys. "These should make your job easier. Report any clue you turn up directly to me."

"Thanks!" Joe said, thrilled to find Meyers had changed his attitude toward them.

The phone on Meyers's desk rang. Meyers nodded at the boys and went to pick it up. Joe took this as a cue that he and Frank should leave. When Frank and Joe were outside in the hall, Joe pulled the badge from his pocket and shined it on his sleeve. "What do you think made Meyers change his mind?" he asked.

"Who knows?" Frank said with a chuckle. "But let's run with it."

Frank and Joe hurried out of the rec hall and headed back to the parking lot. There wasn't much time before they were supposed to meet David Kennedy.

Bayport's airport was just inside the city limits, and it took only ten minutes to reach it. They parked the van and headed inside the terminal. Kennedy's plane wasn't due for another twenty minutes. When they got to the gate, the Hardys found a loud, bustling crowd. The area was crammed with TV crews and photographers, all jostling for position.

"I can't believe Kennedy brings out the media like this, even in a small town like Bayport," Frank said. "There are crews here all the way from New York City. Can't blame Kennedy for wanting to keep away from all this."

By the time Kennedy's plane landed, the crowd had swelled. It completely blocked the area in front of the gate. Joe started to worry. It was their job to help Kennedy avoid the media, but how were they going to get him past this crowd?

Frank must have guessed what was on Joe's mind. The older Hardy was craning his neck and starting to push toward the gate. "Looks like we're going to need a suit of armor to get through this crowd," Frank said. "Got any ideas?"

"I think I do," Joe said. He pulled the badge that Meyers had given him out of his pocket. "Maybe these will help." He attached the badge to his jacket, and Frank put on his as well.

"Nice going," Frank said with a smile. "Let's try to get closer."

As Kennedy and his coach stepped into the gate area, cameras started whirring and flashing. The media pressed forward, asking questions and poking microphones in Kennedy's face.

Kennedy gave a brief interview. While he

spoke, he pushed back his curly dark hair and gazed at the reporters with his intense blue eyes. Frank noticed he looked impatient and a little bit bored. When Kennedy finished, he looked anxiously around.

"Over here!" Joe called out, pushing his way to Kennedy's side. Frank was right behind. "We're your drivers," Joe said. "I'm Joe Hardy. This is my brother, Frank."

"Nice to meet you." Kennedy looked relieved. "Now get me out of here."

Ivan Petrovich, Kennedy's coach, fended off the reporters while Frank and Joe escorted the star through the airport. They quickly loaded Kennedy's luggage into the van and whisked him into the backseat.

"I'm glad that's over," Kennedy said as they pulled out of the parking lot.

"Is it like this wherever you go?" Joe asked.

"Always," Kennedy said, letting out a long sigh. "I hate it!"

"Let's not forget that all the media attention gives you worldwide recognition," Petrovich said. "And that's good for your career."

"Yeah, yeah, yeah," David said with a dismissive wave of his hand. "I don't want recognition, I just want to skate."

"But your fans—" Petrovich began.

"If I have to sign one more autograph, I think

my hand is going to fall off," David said, interrupting his coach. Clearly, the skater had had enough of fame, Frank thought.

On the way to the hotel, Joe took Kennedy's mind off the media by telling him about the festival. The young skater's face lit up as they talked about the various sporting events.

"That sounds like a lot of fun," Kennedy said. "Would you guys mind if I tagged along?"

"That would be great," Joe said. "But aren't you afraid of being mobbed by the crowd?"

"Not if they don't recognize me," Kennedy said. With that, he pulled a red baseball cap from his pocket and settled it in place. "With this cap on, and minus my costume, I look like just another John Doe. It's my version of an optical illusion."

Joe looked in the rearview mirror and was amazed at the transformation. Gone was the intense blue-eyed David Kennedy. In his place was an ordinary teenager with an awkward smile.

"How do I look?" David asked.

"Like any old kid," Joe confirmed.

But Ivan Petrovich bristled. "David, I don't know why you are planning all this fun and games. You know you need to rest. You have a press conference at noon and a practice session later today. We have a schedule to keep."

"Well, I just added something to the schedule," Kennedy said. "I'm going to the festival."

Ivan looked troubled as they pulled up in front of the hotel. "Don't worry, we'll keep an eye on him," Joe said.

Petrovich took one last look at David and waved his finger at him in warning. "Don't do anything foolish. You need to be in top form for the closing ceremonies."

"Aye, aye," David said, giving the coach a mock salute under his cap. "Now let's get going," he said to Frank and Joe, "Before Ivan decides to lock me up in my hotel room."

The boys left the van at the hotel and walked the two blocks to the park. When they reached Park Avenue, icicles as long as three or four feet hung from the overhangs in front of the shops. David laughed and joked with the Hardys as they strolled along, sampling treats from the booths. At the end of a block they found the ice-sculpting competition under way. Joe thought the one of a bald eagle, with wings spread and talons poised, was the best. Frank preferred the bigger-than-life one of Abe Lincoln, including tails and top hat.

The boys were about to leave the demonstration when Joe spotted Craig Thompson standing at a nearby booth. Before Joe could react, Thompson launched two rock-hard snowballs in quick succession.

"Look out!" Joe cried, ducking.

The snowballs missed Frank, Joe, and David, and thumped against the roof of the booth. The icicles hanging there jittered from the blow. Joe stood up and raised his fist at Thompson, sure that the danger was over. But Frank yanked on Joe's arm and dragged him back down.

"What's the matter?" Joe started to say.

Just then, a ten-foot section of icicles broke loose, dropping a shower of needle-sharp missiles that were coming straight at them!

5 Hit and Run

"Watch out!" Frank yelled, dragging Joe away from the icicles. As he did he pushed Kennedy out of the way, toward the street. The icicles hit the sidewalk just beyond them, shattering into a thousand sharp pieces.

The air filled with the sounds of excited voices and footsteps as people hurried to the scene.

Frank glanced at David, who looked shaken. "Are you okay?" Frank asked.

Before David could answer, Frank heard a shriek from down the block.

"Stop, thief!" a woman shouted.

Frank looked down the street in time to see a man running away from a booth selling hand-knitted sweaters. He was built like Chet, wore a maroon jacket, and had a white ski mask pulled down over his face.

"The robber!" Joe cried. "Hurry!"

"What robber?" Kennedy asked, perplexed. But Frank and Joe were already halfway down the block.

Frank's heart was pounding from the cold and the excitement. They were this close to catching the thief!

Joe was in the lead and gaining when the thief darted into a narrow alley. A moment later, Joe and Frank trailed him into the alley.

"It's empty!" Joe cried, stopping short in frustration.

"Look!" Frank pointed to the other end of the alley, which opened onto a larger walkway backing the shops along Park Avenue. "Come on!"

When the Hardys reached the walkway, Frank looked to his right, then his left. This alley ran the length of the block and opened onto the street at each end. There hadn't been time for the man to reach either end yet, but no one was in sight.

"He must have gone in the back door of one of the shops," Joe suggested.

"Probably," Frank said, panting from the chase. "But which one?"

Frank raced to the first door on his right and tried it. It was locked. He was headed toward the second door when David Kennedy came into the alley.

"We lost him!" Joe shouted. "But we think he must have gone in one of these doors. Check the other side of the alley, Frank."

Quickly Frank checked the doors on the left, while Joe and David tried all the doors on the right. "They're all locked," Frank said.

"So are these," Joe answered. "What now?"

"If he went through one of the shops, he's probably back on Park Avenue," Frank said.

"But how'd he get in?" Joe pointed out. "All these doors are locked."

"Good point. Let's see if he's reappeared out on the street," Frank said.

Kennedy tailed along as the Hardys hurried back down the alley. The Hardys quickly explained to him that there'd been a robbery the night before, and that they'd been assigned to the security force. When they stepped onto Park Avenue, Frank scanned the milling crowd. He didn't see anyone answering the description of the thief.

"Where'd he go?" Joe asked. "Do you think he's still hiding in one of the shops?"

"There's only one way to find out," Frank said. "Let's split up. Why don't you start at that end of the block? I'll take this end."

Kennedy's eyes widened. "Can I go with Joe? This is exciting."

Frank's mouth spread in a wide smile. "I don't see why not."

Frank worked his way along the block, checking out every shop. No luck. None of the owners or shopkeepers had seen anyone rushing through their store from the back walkway toward Park Avenue. Frank was down to one last store, Leona Turner's gift shop. The shop was empty, but Frank heard a man and a woman talking in the back.

"Be right with you," Leona called.

Frank glanced around the shelves of her shop while he waited. They were nearly bare, he noticed, as if she couldn't afford to stock them. Finally, Leona pushed a curtain aside and entered the shop. "Thanks for waiting," she said. "What can I do for you?"

"One of the booths at the festival was robbed," Frank said.

"Which one?" Leona asked, a worried expression on her face. "When?"

"The sweater booth. Five, ten minutes ago," Frank said.

"That's Betty's booth!" Leona cried out.

"Did a man come through your back door just now?" Frank asked.

"You don't really think the thief passed through here, do you?" Leona asked, shocked.

"It's possible," Frank said. "Mind if I have a look in your back room, in case he's hiding?"

Leona squared her shoulders, standing every inch of her five feet ten. "I certainly do mind. What's back there is none of your business."

Leona looked flustered as she glanced at her watch. It was gold, decorated with onyx and diamonds. Frank remembered seeing one like it at the mall when he was shopping for a birthday present for his mother. He couldn't remember exactly how much it cost, but he knew it was expensive.

"I'd better go over to the festival to make sure Betty's all right," Leona said. "You'll have to leave with me. I'm going to close the shop for a few minutes."

As Frank followed her from the store, he couldn't help wondering if Leona Turner had something to hide. Who was in the back room? When he stepped onto Park Avenue, Joe and David Kennedy were there. Leona greeted Roger Pender, who emerged from his store, which was next to hers. Both the shop owners locked their doors and headed over to the festival. After they were gone, Frank checked in with Joe and David.

"No luck?" Frank guessed.

Joe shook his head. "No one saw a thing. You know, something's still bothering me. How'd our thief get into one of these shops, anyway? We checked all the back doors. All of them were locked."

Frank thought for a moment. Then David Kennedy offered a suggestion. "Maybe someone let him in," he said.

"Maybe," Frank said. "Or maybe he has a key."

46

"That means the thief must work at one of these shops," Joe said.

"Could be." Frank shook his head and thought for a moment. Once again he wondered about both Roger Pender and Leona Turner. He didn't know about Roger, but just now Leona had been pretty firm about getting him out of her shop—pronto. "Let's head back to the sweater booth and see what we can learn there," Frank suggested.

When they reached the sweater booth, Con Riley was there, questioning Betty Wood, the woman who ran the booth. With him was Dan Meyers, along with Josh Adams and Trevor Jones, another guard. Roger Pender and Leona Turner stood by.

"Can you describe the thief?" Riley asked.

"No," Betty said. "He had a ski mask pulled down over his face. Besides, I couldn't take my eyes off his gun. Then there was that commotion down the street."

Frank remembered Craig Thompson's snowball routine. Briefly, he wondered if Craig was in cahoots with the thief. Maybe he had deliberately tried to create a distraction so no one would notice the robber. It was something to consider.

"How much money did he take?" Officer Riley asked.

"We had a good morning," Betty said. "Counting the raffle tickets, there was nearly a thousand dollars."

Officer Riley jotted down the information in his notebook, looking discouraged. "From the description, I'd say it sounds like the same guy who pulled off the robbery last night."

Pender glared at Frank and Joe. "Where's your friend Chet?"

"Home, with his parents," Joe said. "He had nothing to do with the robbery."

Under his breath, Joe said to Frank, "I'm glad Chet decided not to come. At least now they can't pin this robbery on him."

Frank looked over Joe's shoulder toward the entrance to the park and let out a long groan. Chet's parents were strolling onto Park Avenue. "You're wrong. The Mortons are here," he said. "Even if he was at home, Chet won't have anyone to back his alibi."

Con Riley finished questioning Betty, while Frank and Joe briefed Dan Meyers on what they'd learned. When they were done, Kennedy reminded the Hardys that he had to head back to the hotel room. On the way back to the hotel, Kennedy asked Frank and Joe, "Do you guys get involved in stuff like this often? It's pretty exciting!"

Joe grinned. "Not all the time. But we are detectives, and we have solved a mystery or two in our time."

"I know my way to the park now," Kennedy

said, once they'd reached his hotel. "I should be through with my press conference in time to catch the cross-country skiing event. See you there."

Since it was almost noon, the Hardys decided to grab a quick bite and go over what they knew of the case. They left the van where it was and headed across the park to Howie's Hamburgers, where they each ordered the cheeseburger special.

After they'd taken the edge off their appetites, Joe said with a frown, "Something else is bothering me about this case. I don't understand why the thief would risk robbing the booth in broad daylight. It doesn't make sense."

"I wondered that myself," Frank said. "Betty said the thief took nearly a thousand dollars. That's more than most of the booths take in all day long. Maybe he got lucky, but I think he knew which booth made the most cash."

Joe shook his head. "No way. He couldn't know that unless he was working with the festival."

"My point exactly," Frank said. "What if the thief is involved with the festival, or working with someone that is? Remember, whoever threw that rock at us knew we were on the case."

"Someone could be tipping him off," Joe agreed. "But who?"

"Leona Turner, for example," Frank said, telling Joe about how the woman hadn't wanted him

49

to see her back room. "Or Roger Pender. His store is on Park Avenue, too, and he's involved with the festival. We should investigate both of them."

"Leona Turner knows more about the booths than anyone," Joe said, nodding slowly. "But what about a motive? Does she need money?"

"The shelves in her shop are almost empty, but she's wearing a very expensive watch," Frank said. "Remember how Aunt Gertrude said Leona is always broke?"

"And she was in the park last night," Joe said.

"So was Pender," Frank said.

"What about Pender's motive?" Joe asked, taking a last bite of his burger.

"We need to find out," Frank said. "The cross-country skiing event doesn't start for a couple of hours. Why don't we check out the alley and see if we can spot a clue?"

"You're on," Joe said.

On the way back to the park, Frank and Joe ran into Dan Meyers, who was walking toward the rec hall. The Hardys told him they were heading over to the alley to look for clues.

"Good work," said Meyers, giving them his crooked-toothed smile. "Let me know if you come up with anything."

"Sure," Frank said.

Festival goers packed the street as Frank and Joe crossed Park Avenue and headed into the narrow alley. When they reached the alley that ran behind the shops, Frank could see cars whizzing by on the streets at each end. The alley acted like a funnel, and it sounded as if the cars were only a few feet away.

"I'll take this side," Joe said, raising his voice above the noise. Frank nodded and turned to the left.

Inching his way along the alley, examining every piece of litter, every footprint, Frank hoped to find something that would lead them to the thief. He had covered half the distance when he saw a white minivan turn into the alley. It continued on for several yards, then stopped, its engine idling. Assuming it was making a delivery to one of the shops, Frank ignored it and stooped to examine what looked like a billfold buried under the snow and ice in front of a Dumpster.

Using a pocketknife, he pried it free, but it turned out to be a plastic wrapper. He was dropping the wrapper inside the Dumpster when he heard the engine of the white minivan rev up.

Frank turned back and faced the alley. The minivan was only twenty feet away from Joe, and it was picking up speed.

"Joe! Look out!" Frank warned.

Frank looked on in terror as the minivan raced down the alley, heading straight toward Joe.

6 Timber!

Joe heard Frank calling out to him. He turned around just in time to see the van barreling toward him. "Yikes!" Joe screamed.

At the last possible moment, Joe leaped out of the way, slipping in the snow and landing on his backside. His head slammed into the ground and he was momentarily stunned. Before Joe could catch his breath, the driver shifted into reverse and started backing down the alley, his tires spraying snow in all directions.

Frank, looking on from a few feet away, said, "He can't be serious." Did the driver know Joe was lying on the ground only inches from his rear tires? Did he intend to back the car right over Joe?

Frank leaped into action, running over to his brother and grabbing him by the hand. It was difficult for Frank to plant his feet firmly on the snowy ground, but he managed to hoist up his brother, and Joe stood to the side of the alley, a bit dazed. The van continued backing toward them.

Joe finally regained his senses and said, "That guy's a lunatic. He's about to run us over in reverse!"

"Not if I can help it," Frank said through gritted teeth.

The older Hardy stood firmly in the middle of the alley, all set to force the driver to stop. The van continued on its reverse path toward Frank for several yards. Suddenly the driver slammed on the brakes. Frank didn't move a muscle. Seconds later the driver changed gears, stomped on the gas, and tore down the alley—this time in the right direction. A moment later the van swerved around the corner and disappeared.

"I'm glad he decided not to test your nerve," Joe said to his brother. "I didn't get a look at the plate, did you?"

Angry sparks gleamed in Frank's brown eyes. "Couldn't. There was too much mud splattered on it. Are you okay?"

"Yeah. Close one, though," Joe said. "Do you think there's a connection between whoever threw that rock with the note at our van and this guy?"

"Could be," Frank said. "But that means someone's really watching our moves."

"You said it," Joe put in.

"Come to think of it," Frank said, "the driver didn't head for me until I lifted the lid of this Dumpster. He was just hanging out until I got close to it. So I guess the question is, what's in the Dumpster that we're not supposed to find?"

"And why'd he tear off without making sure he didn't stop us?" Joe added.

He turned to the Dumpster behind him, lifted the lid, and reached in. When he turned back to Frank, Joe held a white ski mask in one hand, a maroon goose-down jacket in the other.

"He ditched his outfit," Joe said. "He threw it away back here, and then he must have run through one of the shops. So which one?"

The shop door closest to the Dumpster read Leona's Gift Shop.

"Looks like Leona Turner had a good reason for not wanting you to check out her back room," Joe observed.

"Just because the thief threw his jacket in a Dumpster close to her shop doesn't mean Leona had anything to do with the robberies," Frank said. "We need more than suspicions and circumstantial evidence. We need proof."

Joe sighed. "Somehow I knew you were going to say that. Any ideas?"

"I'd like to know where she got the money for that expensive watch," Frank said, thinking aloud.

"So what are we waiting for? Let's get to the mall," Joe said.

Frank glanced at his watch and shook his head. "We need to take this jacket and ski mask to Meyers in the rec hall. It's two-fifteen now. That won't leave enough time to get to the mall and back before three when the cross-country skiing starts."

"Good point." Joe thought for a moment. "We'll save the mall for later. First, we see Meyers."

The boys retraced their steps through the alley and headed back into the park. Joe held on to the maroon jacket and white ski mask as they followed the footpath around the lake.

"You know, that jacket looks brand-new," Frank observed. "Maybe we can do some legwork and find out where it was bought, and by whom."

Joe opened the collar, looked at the label inside, and smiled at his brother. "Skip the legwork, Frank," he said. "The jacket's from Castleberry's, that new store that opened a couple of blocks from here just last month. All we have to do is head over there and ask about anyone who has bought a maroon ski jacket in the past few weeks."

"Unless there are two thieves at work," Frank observed.

Joe's eyes widened. "You mean a copycat thief? Could be, but I hope not. It would make our job harder."

"You've got that right. Well, at least we've got two clues to check out now," Frank said. "Leona's watch, and the maroon jacket."

The jingle of bells and the clop of a horse's hooves warned them that a sleigh was approaching. Frank fell into line behind Joe, single file, leaving enough room for the sleigh to pass.

Inside the rec hall, Meyers was talking to Josh Adams and Trevor Jones. The head of security looked up from the map of the park spread out on his desk, and said to Frank and Joe, "Be with you in a minute."

Meyers gave some instructions to Jones and Adams. When he was done, the two men left. With the door closed behind them, Meyers turned to the Hardys. "What's up?"

Joe laid the maroon jacket and white ski mask on Meyers's desk. "We found these in a Dumpster in the alley. We think the thief must have ditched them, then blended into the crowd."

"That's not all," Frank said, telling Meyers about the van.

Meyers looked at the jacket thoughtfully a moment, then raised his eyes and studied the boys with an intent stare. "Very interesting."

"We think the thief is either working with the festival or is working with someone who is," Frank said.

Meyers stiffened. "With the festival? Why do you say that?"

"The thief is hitting booths that are making a lot of cash," Joe explained. "We've got three possible suspects. Both Leona Turner and Roger Pender were in the park last night. And both have shops on Park Avenue, close to the booth that was robbed. Also, the mask and jacket were in a Dumpster right outside Turner's shop. The third possibility is that Craig Thompson created a diversion for the second robbery."

Meyers pursed his lips in thought. "Okay. I'll have my men check this out. Anything else?"

"That's it," Frank said.

"Keep up the good work," Meyers said, shuffling the papers on his desk. "I hope you boys are managing to enjoy the festival, too."

"Actually, I'm competing in the cross-country skiing event this afternoon," Frank told him. "It should be fun."

"Good," Meyers said with a smile. "You know what they say about all work and no play."

Outside, Frank decided to get his skis while Joe waited for David Kennedy near where the cross-country skiing event would take place. Joe picked a vantage point on the hill above the lake. Behind him, festival goers began to head toward the cross-country skiing route. Joe had been waiting only a few minutes when he spotted Kennedy.

Joe waved. Kennedy hurried over, his face red and his intense blue eyes sparkling. David wore jeans, heavy snow boots, and a brightly colored sweater. And on his head he wore the same red cap he'd worn earlier. "Boy, this is great," David said. "No cameras, no microphones, no hassle."

"No kidding," Joe said. "You'd better not ever perform in a baseball cap or you'll blow your cover."

Frank Hardy approached, carrying his skis over his shoulder. Chet was at his side. "I got a serious case of cabin fever," Chet said. "It sure is good to get out of the house."

Joe introduced David to Chet. Chet tried to act casual, but Joe could tell he was excited to meet the pro skater. He's probably dying to ask for his autograph, Joe thought with a smile, to add to his collection. But Chet simply said, "How're you doing?" to Kennedy.

The group joined the crowd heading toward the cross-country event. The staging area for the event was located in a small snow-covered meadow nestled between the tubing hill and a ridge line that marked the boundary of the park. Joe found seats for them all, while Frank signed in. Afterward, Frank joined his brother, Chet, and David at the portable bleachers that had been set up for spectators behind the start-finish line.

Frank studied a map of the course, then handed the map and his number to Joe. While Joe pinned Frank's number to his jacket, Frank slipped his feet into his low-cut cross-country boots. When he was done, Frank stood and snapped his toes into the bindings. A line of contestants was already forming where the race would start, and Frank found himself getting a little nervous. It was only an amateur race, but he wanted to win.

Joe pointed out the route to Chet and David. "They groomed some bridle paths for this race," Joe said. "The racers will start here—circle around past the picnic area, and make a big loop past the stables at the other end of the park. When they reach this wooded hill in the middle, they'll turn and head back here for the finish. Except for the trees scattered around, we can see nearly all the race from the top of that hill." He pointed to a small hill on their left.

"Great," David said. "Good luck, Frank."

Joe said a quick goodbye to Frank, who took his place among the racers. They were all at the starting line, stretching and sliding their skis back and forth, checking the wax. Frank slipped his hands through the loops on the end of his poles, took a deep breath, and waited for the gun.

"On your mark. Get set. Go!"

For a brief moment, there was chaos as each skier jockeyed for the best spot. Frank pushed to the front, then took a couple of quick steps to get his long, narrow skis moving. Finally, he was able to settle into the push-slide, push-slide gait of the cross-country skier.

After fifty yards or so, the pack began to string out. Five racers were ahead of Frank, but he kept

59

to his pace, breathing deep each time he took a step. It was a long race, and he didn't want to burn himself out at the start.

The wax on his skis kept him from sliding backward as he climbed the small rise to the top of the meadow. On the way up, Frank passed one of the racers, two others on the way down. There were only two racers in front of him now, but a quick glance over his shoulder told him others were trying to overtake him.

The stables were in sight when Frank passed another skier, leaving only one ahead of him. His legs started to burn as he skied the sweeping curve around the stables and headed for the wooded hill. Frank pushed through the pain, breathing heavily. The course was harder than he'd expected.

And the biggest test was yet to come. He was already tired, and he would have to use the herringbone on the hill. It was a tricky maneuver—first, he'd need a lot of speed to get as far up the hill as possible. Then he'd have to practically run the rest of the way with his skis turned outward.

Frank picked up his pace, pushing for all he was worth. As he passed the last racer, he let out an awesome yell.

"All right!" he cried. He was in first place!

His speed let him glide almost thirty yards up the hill. After that, he pointed the toes of his skis out and began the steep climb. It took all the leg-and-arm strength he could muster, as he practically leapt from foot to foot, trying to get as much distance into each stride as possible.

Frank was breathing hard when he reached the woods at the top of the hill. Just then he heard Joe's voice from a hill high above him, on his right.

"Go, Frank!" Joe said. "You're going to win!"

Along with Joe, David and Chet started shouting their encouragement. Frank glanced back to see a racer only ten yards behind him. A few more turns, then the finish line.

Frank planted his poles and pushed off. He bent his knees, gaining as much speed as he could. Now came a series of turns, the last tricky part of the course. Frank's concentration was fierce as he set himself up for the end of the race.

But as he started into the turn, he heard a loud noise and stiffened. It sounded like a huge crackling clap of thunder.

Startled, Frank looked up—just in time to see a huge pine tree come crashing down in front of him.

7 Runaway

Joe, Chet, and David were still on the hill, about two hundred yards above the course. When the boom rang out, Joe thought it must be a truck backfiring. But he quickly realized they were too deep in the woods to hear any traffic.

"What was that?" Joe asked.

"Look!" Chet said, pointing out someone running through the woods, just off the trail. "Isn't that Craig Thompson?"

Joe didn't get a good look. His eyes had been riveted on the trail, where Frank was skiing. Then David called his attention to a wavering pine tree, just to the side of the trail.

"That tree's going to fall!" David cried out.

Sure enough, a second later, the huge tree went crashing to the ground—right onto the course!

Joe drew in a sharp breath. Frank had disappeared!

"Come on!" Joe urged Chet and David. "We've got to help him. That tree might have pinned him to the ground."

The boys scrambled through the snow, down the steep hill, and toward the fallen tree. When they got to the trail, they found Frank tangled among the branches of the tree. His skis were off, and he was lying on his side. One by one, other skiers from the race cruised to a quick stop, worried expressions on their faces.

Frank opened his eyes and looked up. He sputtered and brushed the snow away from his mouth and eyes as he sat up.

"Frank!" Joe let out a long sigh of relief. He, Chet, and David broke off some of the pine branches that had entangled Frank. Then Joe gave his brother a hand up. "I thought you were squashed, Frank."

"We all did," David added. "You gave us a real scare, Frank."

"Are you all right?" Chet asked.

"Shaken up a little is all," Frank said. "But I'm afraid my skis have had it."

While Frank picked himself up and collected his gear, Joe strode over to the tree's trunk. It was sawn clean, with just a small bit of chipped wood where the final break had happened.

"Just what I thought," Joe called out. "Someone

sawed through this trunk. Whoever it was wanted that tree to fall on you." Joe's eyes caught a glint of metal in the snow next to the trunk. He picked up a metal wedge from near the base of the tree. "That person probably used this wedge to tilt it toward the trail. Then when Frank came along, he gave it a good shove."

"But what about the noise of the saw?" Chet asked. "Wouldn't someone have heard him?"

"It could have been cut when no one was around," David suggested.

"Besides," Joe added, "the crowds have been making a lot of noise that might have masked the sound."

By now a crowd had begun to gather, including the other racers and spectators. Josh Adams came walking up the trail toward them. Roger Pender was at his side. "What happened here? Is everyone all right?" Adams asked.

Quickly, Joe told him about Frank's accident and how Chet had seen someone running away from the trail. Then he showed him where the tree had been cut. Adams pulled a two-way radio from his pocket and repeated to Meyers what Joe had told him. "I want to see the Hardys in my office," Meyers said, then the radio went silent.

Roger Pender raised his voice above the murmur of the crowd. "Sorry, folks. The tree is blocking the trail. The race is over."

With disappointed groans, the crowd and the

64

other racers began making their way back to the start-finish line. "I'll get the grounds crew up here to clear the tree away," Pender said, then turned and followed the crowd.

Frank collected his skis. Then, as a group, Adams, Frank, Joe, Chet, and Kennedy made their way down the hill.

"I've got to head out to a practice session now," David said. "How about if I meet you guys later? We can check out more of the festival. I'd like to buy one of those mugs with the cows on it," he said.

"A cow mug?" Chet repeated, looking curiously at the star skater.

"Yeah," David said a little sheepishly. "My mother is into cows, you know. And her birthday's coming up."

"Okay, we'll see you in a while, then," Frank said.

"And don't have any more of your adventures without me," David added as he walked off.

"I can't believe that guy," Chet said with wide eyes. "He's a world-class athlete, and he thinks our adventures are fun! And he's buying his mother a birthday present. Wow."

Joe smiled and said, "He doesn't seem like such a bad-boy type, does he?" Obviously, David didn't get much excitement in his life—or at least the kind he got being around the Hardys.

Chet left for home, and Joe wandered around

the rec hall while Frank reported to Meyers. Afterward, Joe asked his brother, "Still feel like going to the mall?"

"More than ever," Frank said. "I want to get to the bottom of this. Let's stop at Castleberry's on the way and check out that jacket."

They followed the footpath across the bridge and to the parking lot. As they reached their van, Joe spotted Craig Thompson getting into his car.

"I saw Thompson throw those snowballs earlier today, and I'm pretty sure he tampered with the blade on my skate," Joe said. "Chet thought it was him running away through the woods at the skiing event. Think he cut that tree?"

"It's possible," Frank said. "But it just doesn't feel right. What's his motive?"

Joe narrowed his eyes at Craig. "I don't know, but I intend to find out. We'll keep a low profile with the guy, though. Let's not have him think we suspect him."

While Joe took the wheel, Frank settled back into the passenger seat. Joe turned north on Oak Street. Castleberry's was about halfway down the block.

Inside the shop, Joe was disappointed to see it was a self-service store, with no clerks and at least ten cash registers lined up by the door. The store was doing a booming business, and there were long lines at each register.

"Let's go," Frank said. "There's no way one of

the cashiers would remember who bought a maroon jacket."

Joe wasn't so easily deterred, but ten minutes later, after questioning half of the cashiers, he was willing to admit Frank was right. Too many people were passing in and out of the store. The manager said they'd sold fifty of those maroon ski jackets recently. Discouraged, the Hardys returned to the van. As they were passing Pender's store, Joe saw it was empty.

"Castleberry's can't be good for Pender," he remarked. "The two stores are only a few blocks away from each other."

"Good point," Frank agreed. "You think Pender's business is hurting? That could be a motive for committing those robberies."

"It's something to consider," Joe said, continuing on to the mall. "We'll have to check it out later."

Bayport Center Mall was bustling, even though it was the middle of the week and in the afternoon. An escalator carried Frank and Joe to the second floor. Upstairs, Frank pointed out an exclusive jewelry shop.

"That's it," he said. "That's where I saw a watch like the one Leona was wearing."

They walked inside and approached a glass-topped counter. "May I help you?" the clerk asked.

67

"We're interested in that diamond-and-onyx watch you had displayed in the window last week," Frank said.

The clerk smiled. "Yes. A lovely piece. I'm sorry, but I sold it just this morning."

"That's too bad," Joe said. "We were hoping to buy it for our mother. Maybe the woman who bought it would be interested in selling it? Do you have her name, or an address on the charge slip?"

"A man bought it," the clerk said. "And I'm sorry, but we don't give out names and addresses. We have some other fine watches. Perhaps . . ."

"I'm afraid not," Joe said. "My mom really liked that watch. Thanks anyway."

As soon as they were out of hearing range, Joe turned to Frank and said, in frustration, "So Leona didn't buy the watch. That puts us right back where we started. We have no proof that she's gotten her hands on a ton of money lately."

Frank and Joe were going to meet David at seven, and it was only six. They decided to kill time by eating a couple of tacos at a Mexican restaurant in the mall's food court. Forty-five minutes later, the boys headed back to the park to wait for David. Along the way it began to snow in big fluffy flakes. When they pulled into the lot, Joe looked up the hill toward the Bradford mansion.

"I can't say I blame Bradford's daughter," Joe said with a shiver. "I think I'd run away, too, if I had to live there."

Frank climbed out and locked the van. "It was probably pretty plush in its day."

"If you say so," Joe said. "We'd better hurry. Kennedy's probably waiting for us."

The lights in the trees overhead twinkled as they hurried across the bridge and made their way along the footpath. David was waiting in front of the rec hall when they arrived. Below them, skaters kept time to the music drifting from the lake, while squeals and laughter sounded from the tubing hill. The fresh snow was making the tubing course slippery.

"Want to take one of those sleigh rides?" David asked. "It looks like fun."

"Sure," Joe agreed. "Let's head over to the stables."

Joe and Frank led David along the footpath around the lake, then turned left into a lane wide enough to accommodate a sleigh. After passing through sparsely wooded terrain, they rounded a gentle knoll. A sleigh, drawn by a dapple gray, sat in front of the stable.

As they crossed to the stable, a woman and her small daughter joined three other people who were already in the sleigh.

"Room for one more!" the driver announced. "Any takers?"

"We'll wait for the next one," Joe said.

"Won't be a next one until tomorrow," the driver said. "This is the last one."

Joe noticed that David looked disappointed. "Why don't you go ahead?" Joe asked. "Frank and I will wait here for you."

"You're sure you don't mind?" David asked.

"No problem," Frank said.

"Thanks." David climbed into the sleigh and said, "Don't do anything exciting until I get back!"

As Joe watched the sleigh round the knoll, a loud boom sounded from the direction of the parking lot. "That was a gunshot!" Joe announced, looking toward the parking lot.

"Let's go!" Frank was about to race off in the direction of the shot, when the dapple gray in the front of the sleigh reared and pawed the air, throwing the driver.

The horse's hooves hit the ground. He whinnied and took off like a bolt, rocketing away at breakneck speed.

8 Seeing Stars

As the driverless sleigh took off, it tipped on one runner, then slammed to the ground again. The passengers began to scream for help. But the horse was still galloping away at breakneck speed.

The sleigh could tip over, maybe even crash, and Frank knew he didn't have a second to lose.

"We'll never outrun that horse!" Frank shouted. "We've got to cut him off somehow."

"You're right," Joe shot back. "But how?"

Frank scanned the terrain. The horse had taken a winding path that would eventually end up between two hills. "Up there!" Frank cried, pointing to a direct route to the top of one of the hills.

Together, the Hardys raced up the hill. Down below, through the falling snow, Frank saw the

71

sleigh come around the bend. There was panic in the horse's wide white eyes. With head raised, ears laid back, and nostrils flaring, he barreled around the curve. The sleigh caromed off a snow-bank, bounced on both runners, then tilted the other way, slamming Kennedy and the other passengers from side to side.

Frank charged down the slope, half running, half sliding in the snow. Joe was right behind.

Pausing on a rock outcropping, Frank waited for the horse to reach him. When the gray was directly below the rock, Frank took a flying jump into the air. He managed to straddle the animal and get one hand clamped on the harness. The horse was startled by Frank's weight dropping on him from out of nowhere, and he reared up and whinnied. Frank fell off the horse but managed to hold on to the harness. The horse had lost his momentum but was determined to race on. After being dragged along for several yards, Frank's grip on the harness started slipping. Frantically, he tried to grab hold with his other hand, while at the same time digging his heels into the snowy ground.

Out of the corner of his eye, Frank saw Joe dive for the rear of the sleigh. His brother's weight acted like a rudder and helped steady the sleigh. Frank was finally able to get both hands on the harness. He yanked the horse's head down. The gray planted his front legs and came to a screeching halt. Still panicked, he snorted, stomped the ground, and tried to rear.

Frank kept a firm grip on the harness. "Whoa, boy. Whoa. It's all right," he said in a low soothing voice.

"Whew," Joe said, hurrying to the side of the sleigh. "Is everyone all right?"

Several passengers nodded silently, while others began to step down from the sleigh, eager to escape the runaway horse. The horse pricked his ears and tried again to rear. "Better get them out of the sleigh," Frank said to Joe.

David Kennedy, his face white, was the last one off. Just as he was stepping down from the sleigh, the driver came rushing up the path. "I can't believe it!" the driver cried. "He never bucks like that. Is everyone all right?"

"Thanks to Frank and Joe they are," David said. "Boy, am I sorry I took you up on your offer to be the last one in that sleigh," he added with a laugh.

"It's because of that backfire," the driver said. "That's what made him bolt."

"That was no backfire," Frank said. "It was a gunshot."

The driver's eyes widened. "A gunshot? Why would someone fire a gun in the park?"

"Good question," Joe said.

"We'd better check it out," Frank said. Eager to investigate, he asked the sleigh driver, "Is there a flashlight in the stable?"

73

"There are a couple of them on the workbench in the tack room," the driver said.

The three boys went to the stable. Frank ran in and came back with the flashlight. Then the boys headed in the direction where the shot had come from: a parking lot off to the side of the stables. They had traveled only fifty feet or so when Frank stopped and turned the flashlight on. It lit up the large flakes of snow falling faster and thicker through the air.

"What are we looking for?" David asked.

"Footprints mostly," Joe said as Frank shone the beam along the snow-covered ground.

"Over here," Frank said in excitement. "There's a fresh set of prints. The snow hasn't covered them yet. Be careful. Don't mess them up."

Joe and David hurried over. Frank pointed out the trampled patch of snow, then directed the light toward the stable. They could all see the area in front of it clearly.

"Looks like someone stood here awhile. He left in a hurry." Frank shone the light along a trail of prints leading toward the parking lot.

"How can you tell?" David asked.

"He was walking, taking his time when he came this way," Frank said, pointing the light to a second line of prints. "These prints are two feet apart. The others are four feet apart, and deeper, which is a sure sign he was running."

"Whew. There's more to being a detective than I thought," David said.

"There's not much point in following the prints to the parking lot," Joe said. "He's probably long gone. Why don't we follow this other set and see where he came from?"

"Good idea," Frank said. "Maybe we'll learn something."

As the boys followed the line of prints from tree trunk to tree trunk, Frank noticed the prints always kept ten or twelve feet off to the side of the lane. "Looks like whoever followed us went to a lot of trouble to keep out of sight," Frank said.

When they reached the footpath, the prints ended, blending in with hundreds of others.

"Do you think the guy who cut down that tree took a shot at us?" Joe asked.

"It's possible, but if he did, he's a lousy shot," Frank said. "All he did was scare the horse."

The Hardys investigated for a while longer, but didn't turn up any more clues. By then it was almost eight-thirty. David decided to head back to his hotel room, promising to see them the next night at the speed-skating rink. Frank and Joe went over to the rec hall to report what they'd found to Dan Meyers.

At Meyers's office, Dan was just finishing up for the day as Frank and Joe stepped into the room.

"Thought you should know someone fired a gun in the park," Frank said.

"A gun!" Meyers said. "When? Was anyone hurt?" Meyers listened carefully as Frank and Joe told him about the gunshot and the runaway horse. When they were done, Meyers said, "Jones and Adams are out on patrol. I'll radio this in to them and have them check it out. Thanks, boys. You're doing great."

As Frank and Joe stepped into the hall, Frank heard the two-way radio on Meyers's desk crackle. "That must be Meyers contacting Jones and Adams," Frank remarked.

Neither Frank nor Joe said anything until they were in the van, then Joe turned to his brother. "You know, I'd feel a whole lot better if I knew what was going on."

"I know what you mean," Frank said. "Did whoever fired that gun just want to spook the horse? Why?" The questions piled up in Frank's mind. "We know Leona Turner didn't buy that watch herself, so maybe she didn't steal the money. But why was the maroon jacket and ski cap in the Dumpster behind her store? And what about Roger Pender?"

Frank let out a long sigh as Joe drove them home. This was the part of the case Frank hated the most—the part where nothing seemed to make any sense.

When the boys walked into their kitchen fifteen minutes later, Aunt Gertrude, visibly upset,

76

jumped up from the table. "There's been another robbery," she said.

"When? Where?" Frank asked.

"Around twenty minutes ago, on Park Avenue again," Aunt Gertrude answered. "The hot-dog booth."

Frank turned to Joe. "That was fast," he said. "We were with Meyers twenty minutes ago. It must have happened right after we left."

"You know, Frank, what if the gunshot was a diversion?" Joe suggested slowly. "A ploy to keep us occupied."

"Gunshot?" Aunt Gertrude gasped. "What gunshot?"

Frank told her about the gunshot and the runaway horse.

"Diversion or not, the robber has found a source of ready cash in the festival," Aunt Gertrude said. "And I don't mind telling you, it has me worried. If it keeps up, attendance will drop. Then we'll never raise enough money."

"I'd like to question whoever was in the booth about the robbery," Frank said.

"It was Liz Benson. I'm sure she'd be willing to help. I'll call her," Aunt Gertrude said, crossing to the kitchen phone. She dialed, and after explaining what the boys wanted, Aunt Gertrude listened a moment, then said, "Hold on. I'll ask them."

She turned to the boys. "Liz says to stop by her

house tomorrow. She'll talk to you then. Right now she's a little upset."

"We'll meet with her tomorrow, then," Frank said. Turning to Joe, he said, "I think now might be a good time to go investigate the booth that was robbed. No one's around, so we can get a better look."

"Good idea," Joe said. Without even taking off their jackets, the boys turned around and headed back out.

They arrived on Park Avenue about twenty minutes later. The street was deserted, the shops closed and dark.

When they reached the hot-dog booth, Joe looked at the booth next door. It was the sweater booth that had been robbed earlier. He nodded toward the shops of Leona Turner and Roger Pender, right across the way.

"Opportunity, again," Joe said. "Don't you think it's looking more and more like one of them is involved? I know Leona Turner is at the top of my list."

"You may be right," Frank said.

He and Joe searched the area, which was lit up by the streetlights. Nothing unusual stood out, and they began to consider calling it a night.

"Looks like Liz Benson forgot to empty her trash," Joe said.

"I'll empty it for her," Frank said.

He picked up the basket and carried it through

the narrow alley to the big alley behind the shops. He was tilting it into the Dumpster when he heard a noise behind him. Frank's back muscles tightened. Before he could turn around, something hit him on the back of the head. For an instant Frank saw dazzling stars. Then everything went black.

9 Close Shave

Joe heard a garbage truck turn into the alley as he circled the booth one more time. Growing cold in the dark night, Joe shivered under his jacket as he headed toward the alley to see what was keeping Frank. It was so cold that Joe could see his breath when he reached the back alley. He saw the garbage truck pulled up nose first in front of the Dumpster. But where was Frank? The mechanical arms on either side of the truck were lowered toward the Dumpster.

As Joe approached, the driver hopped out of the cab and attached the arms to the brackets on the side of the Dumpster. Then he punched a button in the control panel located on the side of the truck and hopped back into the cab.

Joe watched the arms swing the bulky Dumpster to the back of the truck. With a clang, the arms stopped, tilting the Dumpster upside down and emptying the trash into the back of the truck.

"Frank, where are you?" Joe called as he continued along the dark alley.

The sound of the compactor was deafening. Joe was about to turn around when he spotted the booth's trash basket beside the Dumpster.

"Frank!" Joe cried, realizing instantly that something was wrong. He ran to the side of the garbage truck and threw the emergency lever. With a slow grinding of gears and a great squeal, the truck's compactor stopped.

Immediately, the driver called out to Joe. "What're you doing, kid? Why'd you stop my truck?

"Frank? Are you in there?" Joe called down into the compactor, ignoring the driver.

"Get me out of here," came Frank's frantic answer. "I'm stuck!"

Joe jumped onto the rear bumper, leaned inside, and spotted Frank. His older brother was covered in garbage. There were heaps of refuse between Frank and Joe, but Joe was able to reach Frank's hand and help him slowly work his way out of the truck.

The driver, standing beside the truck, watched openmouthed as Frank emerged from the compactor. "What on earth do you kids think you're doing? Garbage trucks can be dangerous. You're not supposed to goof off around them!"

"We weren't goofing off, believe me," Frank explained, dusting the garbage from his clothes. "Someone knocked me out and threw me into that Dumpster. You were about to flatten me into lunch meat!"

The truck driver turned white. "I'm sorry, kid," he said. "I had no idea! Are you all right?"

"I'm okay," Frank said. "A little bruised, but otherwise, fine."

"That's all relative," Joe said, pinching his nose. "Unharmed—maybe. Stinky—most definitely."

As they walked back to the van, Joe asked Frank, "Did you see who hit you?"

"No. I didn't even hear whoever it was until it was too late," Frank said. "I guess the snow muffled his footsteps."

"Or *hers*," Joe said. "That Dumpster is right outside Leona Turner's back door. She could have been in the back of the shop. Maybe she saw you out there and decided it was a good time to put you out with the trash."

"Very funny," Frank said. "Or maybe Pender noticed me."

"Possibly." Joe drove the van out of the parking lot. "One thing we haven't discussed is the possibility that Pender and Turner are working together. Those were a man's tracks in the snow over by the stable. Leona Turner's a big woman, but I can't picture her chopping down a tree or tossing you into a Dumpster."

"Good point," Frank said. "Maybe the man who bought the watch is involved. Why don't we call the jewelry-store clerk tomorrow? Maybe he can describe him."

"Good idea," Frank said. "While we're at it, I'd like to find out more about both Pender and Turner. Let's stake out both their shops tomorrow. I'll take Leona's, you take Pender's."

"You're on," said Joe. "Now let's get home— and fast. Someone here needs a shower, and I'll give you a hint: it's not me."

The next morning, after the boys finished the French toast Aunt Gertrude had cooked for them, Frank called the jewelry shop. He asked the clerk if he could describe the man who bought the watch. "As a matter of fact, I can," the clerk said. "He came back in after you boys left and bought a diamond-and-sapphire ring. He's in his early forties, around five eight or nine, and slim. He has dark hair, gray at the temples, and wears gold-rimmed glasses."

Frank felt his disappointment rise. The person the clerk described wasn't Pender. Roger was young, didn't have gray hair, and didn't wear glasses, as far as Frank knew. He thanked the clerk, and after replacing the receiver, he told Joe what he'd learned.

Joe shook his head. "That's not Pender. So who is it?"

"Leona Turner was wearing a ring like that last night," Aunt Gertrude said. "I must say I wondered how she could afford it. She must have a wealthy admirer. . . . Interesting." Aunt Gertrude nodded slowly. "Well, anyway. Here's Liz Benson's address. I told her you'd stop by this morning, remember."

"I remember," Frank said, glancing at the address. Liz Benson lived close to the high school, between the Hardys' place and the park. "We can stop by on our way over to the park."

The boys bundled up, scraped the newly fallen snow off the van's windows, and climbed in. Joe had his skates with him. The speed-skating event was that night, and no matter what happened on the case, Joe would be ready to race.

Five minutes later Frank was pulling up to the curb in front of Liz Benson's house. The boys walked to the front door and rang the bell. Ms. Benson, a small, energetic woman, opened the door on the second ring.

"Can I help you?" she asked.

The boys introduced themselves. "I'm Frank Hardy, and this is my brother, Joe."

"Of course," Ms. Benson said, her face spreading into a grin. "Come on in."

Inside, Liz Benson motioned them to the living room. Frank and Joe sat on the sofa, while Ms.

Benson perched on the edge of a chair. "Where do we start?" she asked.

"We'd like to know everything you can remember about the robbery," Frank said, removing his notebook and pen.

"There's not much to tell," Liz Benson said with a sigh. "It was cold. The crowd had thinned out, and I was staying as close to the heater as possible. I didn't notice the man until he waved a gun in my face and ordered me to hand over the cash. Counting the raffle-ticket sales, he took nearly fifteen hundred dollars." She paused. "I feel so terrible! Is there anything you can do?"

"Can you describe him?" Joe asked.

"Not very well. He had on a black ski mask with red and white stars on it pulled down over his face. His jacket was white, with a navy blue stripe down the arm."

Frank took a note of her description. It wasn't the same outfit the thief had worn before. "Was he short or tall? Fat or thin?" Frank asked.

"Tall and thin," she said. "Taller than both of you."

Frank stood six feet one. Joe was only an inch shorter.

"Did you see which way he went?" Joe asked.

"Yes," she said. "He darted into the alley. I ran into Leona's shop and called the police. I'm afraid that's all I can tell you."

Frank and Joe stood. "Thanks for your help,"

Frank said. "If you remember anything else, please call."

"I'll do that," Liz Benson assured them. As soon as she closed the door behind them, Joe turned to Frank. "At least they can't blame this one on Chet. He's not tall and thin."

Frank opened the van door and climbed behind the steering wheel. "You're right," he said. "There seems to be a second criminal operating here. But it complicates matters. We don't know if last night's robbery was a copycat, or if we're facing a gang of thieves."

"Maybe we should check in and find out what Meyers knows about this latest robbery," Joe suggested.

"Good idea," Frank said, nosing the van into traffic. It was snowing lightly when the Hardys reached the park fifteen minutes later. They crossed the bridge and headed to the rec hall and Meyers's office. The security chief was free and quickly motioned for Frank and Joe to take a seat. He had a sip of his coffee and said, "What gives? I suppose you heard about our latest robbery? I got the call from Adams just as you were leaving yesterday. Since we could handle it ourselves, I thought I'd let you boys go on home."

"I understand," Frank said. Then he told Meyers about the attack in the alley the night before. "Meanwhile, we've already questioned Liz Benson about the robbery. She says the thief was tall and thin and wore a white jacket. The last thief was short and husky. That means that either there's more than one thief, or we're up against a gang. Joe and I have a theory that someone connected with the festival could be giving the thieves tips—letting them know when a booth has the most money."

Meyers nodded. "I've doubled the guards around the booths, but it isn't helping." He paused, rubbing his chin thoughtfully. "I know you guys have been busy. Have you had a chance to check out Leona Turner or Roger Pender?"

"Not yet, but we intend to," Frank said.

"Good. Let me know what you find out," Meyers said. As he turned to the paperwork on his desk, he gave them a crooked smile. "And thanks for all your hard work. I really appreciate it."

"No problem," Frank said.

Out in the rec hall, Frank spotted Adams and Jones, who were drinking coffee. Leona Turner was also there, talking to a man in the chestnut booth. Roger Pender sat at a table with a cup of coffee and a soft pretzel in front of him.

"Don't you think it's strange that we always see them together?" Frank pointed out to Joe.

"Or that Craig Thompson and his buddies are here, too?" Joe added, tilting his head in the direction of the soda machines, where Craig and the others were hanging out. "Are they following us, or what?" Joe wondered aloud.

Just then Aunt Gertrude came into the rec hall, her arms loaded down with decorations. "Frank, Joe, can you come here? I need your help."

Frank and Joe walked over to a table where Aunt Gertrude set down her decorations. "What's up?" Frank asked.

"I've been taken off my booth and put in charge of decorating the rec hall for the dance tomorrow night," Gertrude explained. "I wanted to put up some holly and evergreen boughs. Mr. Jenkins said we can cut all we need free of charge from that patch of woods he owns south of town. Would you mind?"

Frank and Joe exchanged a look. They were on a case, and they didn't exactly feel like interrupting the investigation to help with interior decoration. But Aunt Gertrude's expression was so eager and hopeful, how could they turn her down?

"Sure," Frank said, trying to sound enthusiastic.

They zipped up their jackets and headed out toward Dan Jenkins's place. Luckily, they kept tools in the van, so they already had a hatchet and tarp.

It was snowing hard as Frank parked by Jenkins's woods. The snow was deep and icy under the trees. As they gathered holly and fir, Frank heard the sound of an ax in the distance.

"Mr. Jenkins must be cutting firewood," Frank said, dropping an evergreen bough on the tarp.

The snowfall thickened as the boys worked. The

sound of the ax had stopped when, thirty minutes later, the tarp was piled high with evergreen branches and sprigs of holly. The sharp, pleasant odor of resin filled the air as Joe dropped his hatchet on the tarp.

"Looks like enough," Joe said. "I'll take the front end. You get the back."

The boys picked up the corners of the tarp and headed toward their van. They'd gone only forty feet or so when Frank heard a strange whooshing sound.

He looked up and saw a two-bladed ax sailing through the air. The glinting axhead shot like a missile through the air, staying fixed on its deadly course toward Frank's head.

10 A Near Miss

"Duck!" Joe yelled to Frank as he dropped to the ground. The ax whizzed by Frank's head, missing by only inches, and sank into the trunk of an evergreen with a resounding thud. Frank heard it twang as it vibrated in the tree. It was at eye level and only a foot away from him—much too close for comfort.

Joe scrambled to his feet and took a deep breath. "That was a close shave," he said.

"Shhh! Listen," Frank said, holding a finger to his lips.

The air was still. In the near distance, a dead branch snapped. A moment later Joe heard the muffled sound of running footsteps.

"Over there," Frank whispered, pointing to

their left. Joe turned in time to catch a shadowy glimpse of a husky man running through the trees.

"Let's go," Joe said, tearing into action.

The boys raced into the woods after the guy. They were gaining on their quarry when Joe lost sight of the man behind a thick stand of evergreens. "Where'd he go?" Joe said, stopping to catch his breath. The evergreens surrounded them, creating a maze in the forest, and Joe had completely lost his bearings.

Frank shook his head and shrugged.

In the quiet woods, Joe listened intensely. Suddenly, he heard a car door slam, followed by the sound of an engine.

"This way!" Joe shouted. "Quick."

Joe darted through the woods, slapping snow-laden branches out of his way and jumping over fallen trees and rocks. Frank was close behind, and soon they reached a narrow back road. Just as they stepped onto the road, Joe spotted the taillights of a white minivan.

"That's the same guy who tried to run us down in the alley behind Leona's and Pender's stores!" Joe announced.

Before either of the Hardys could react, the van swerved around a corner and disappeared. Frustrated, Joe snatched his cap off and threw it on the ground.

"That ax was no accident," Joe said.

"You're right," Frank said. "And whoever threw it knew we were going to be out here."

"Was it someone in the rec hall?" Joe asked. "Or someone who followed us out here?"

"Good question. Leona Turner was at the rec hall," Frank pointed out. "So were Roger Pender and Craig Thompson. And Thompson is built like Chet."

"I think it's time we did some serious investigation of Leona and Pender," Joe said. "Let's get the evergreens and head back."

On the way back to the park, Frank thought aloud as Joe drove. "I'm convinced we're dealing with more than one person. Remember that gunshot? The robbery happened soon after. That could have been one person acting alone, but chances are it was two people working together."

"Don't forget that Craig caused that first diversion with the snowball," Joe pointed out. "And that guy in the woods just now was big, like Craig."

"Maybe," Frank said, thinking for a moment. "But if Craig was working with the thief, why would he be so obvious about throwing that snowball? Wouldn't he want to keep a lower profile?"

"I guess," Joe admitted.

When the boys reached the park, they hauled the tarp of evergreens out of the van and headed across the bridge toward the rec hall. About halfway there, they ran into Chet, who helped them drag the evergreens the rest of the way. Inside, Aunt Gertrude was blowing up balloons. She stopped for a moment and led the boys to the supply room. After they unloaded the tarp, the boys returned to the main room in the rec hall.

"Boy, those hot dogs smell good," Chet said.

"You're right, they do," Frank said, and turned to Joe. "How about a lunch break before we head over to Pender's and Leona's shops?"

"Sounds good," Joe agreed.

Five minutes later Chet, Joe, and Frank were all seated around a table, chowing down on hot dogs, potato chips, and cold sodas. Between bites, Frank told Chet about the attack in the woods. Chet's eyes went wide when he heard about the ax and the guy in the white minivan.

"It sounds like someone wants to seriously scare you away," Chet said.

"Well, that's not going to happen," Joe said, standing up to throw away his trash. "Come on, Frank. It's time to check out Leona and Pender, once and for all."

The Hardys left Chet at the tubing hill, then headed out toward Park Avenue to check out Leona's and Pender's shops. It had stopped snowing by the time they reached Park Avenue, but the sky was still gray. As they crossed the street, Joe saw a man wearing gold-rimmed glasses enter Leona's shop.

"Hey, Frank," Joe said, pulling his brother back. "Think that's the guy who bought the watch and ring?"

"Could be," Frank said. "He matches the description—early forties, graying hair. See what you can find out," Frank said. "I'll check out Pender's shop."

Joe took a deep breath. "Right," he said, and opened the door of Leona's shop.

No one was out front, but he heard voices in the back room. "Then everything's all set," the man said.

"Yes. The festival ends day after tomorrow. I've got the plane tickets," Leona answered. "My lease is up at the end of the month. And the shop at the mall agreed to take any stock that's left off my hands."

Wow, Joe thought. Unless he was wrong, Leona Turner was planning her getaway! As he tiptoed toward the curtain, his foot brushed a flimsy display rack. It toppled to the floor with a loud clatter.

Leona brushed the curtains aside, rushed into the shop, and glared at Joe. "Joe Hardy! What on earth? Look at the mess you just made."

The man with the gold-rimmed glasses stepped through the curtain and sat the rack upright. "It doesn't matter, darling," he said. "This time next week we'll be in Paris, France, on our honeymoon. Leave the boy alone."

94

Leona looked at the sapphire-and-diamond ring on her finger and smiled. "You're right, of course. I'm so happy about getting married, nothing can spoil it!"

"You're getting married?" Joe asked, swallowing his surprise.

"Isn't it wonderful?" Leona said, her eyes beaming.

"Yeah, right," Joe said, trying not to be so obviously disappointed. He'd just lost his prime suspect! Obviously, Leona's watch and the ring were gifts. And her shelves were bare because she was going out of business, not because she couldn't afford to keep them stocked.

"Was there something you needed, Joe?" Leona asked. "Or were you just browsing?"

At Pender's sporting goods shop, Roger Pender stood at the counter of the empty store, talking on the phone. His back was to the door, giving Frank the perfect opportunity to eavesdrop. He gently eased the door shut behind him and walked slowly toward the counter.

"If you don't let me have that shipment, I might as well close my doors," Pender was saying. There was a pause. "But I've told you. I can't pay you right now. I don't have the money."

Frank rummaged through the ski masks and mittens piled on the table. He remembered what a bustling business Castleberry's had been doing the day before. It sounded as if the new store really was eating into Roger's business. Frank couldn't wait to tell Joe that he had evidence to support a motive for Roger Pender.

"Be that way," Pender said, and slammed the receiver down.

Frank coughed slightly to let Pender know he was there. Pender spun around. "Oh, hello, Frank. I didn't hear you come in." He gave a weak smile. "Guess you heard the news. Castleberry's is going to ruin me. I'd hoped the festival would bring some business into the shop, but so far it hasn't happened."

Frank spotted a white ski mask with a blue lightning bolt on the table. Close by was a black one with blue and red stars. He picked up the black mask and walked to the counter.

"I'm trying to get to the bottom of these robberies," Frank said, deciding to be direct with Pender. "Joe and I think the robber has access to one of the shops along Park Avenue. The thief disappeared into the alley behind your store after the second robbery. Have you seen anyone suspicious hanging around any of the shops?"

"No, but I wish you'd hurry up and find the guy," Pender said with a sigh. "It's hurting festival attendance, and I don't think my business can take any more strain."

"We'll do what we can," Frank said. He went to pay for the ski maks. As Pender rang up the sale,

96

Frank asked, "Do any of the shop owners drive a white minivan?"

Pender dropped the ski mask into a bag and handed it to Frank, a puzzled expression on his face. "Not that I know of. Why?"

"Just curious," Frank said. "Well, thanks anyway." As he turned toward the door, Craig Thompson rushed into the shop.

"Roger, I—" At the sight of Frank Hardy, Craig came to a screeching halt. He looked nervously at Frank, then at Pender.

"I was just leaving," Frank said with a small grin. He knew there was no point in sticking around. But he thought it was awfully curious that Thompson seemed upset to see Frank in Roger's store. Frank stepped outside, eager to share his news with Joe.

The younger Hardy was waiting for Frank across the street. As the boys headed back to the park, Frank told Joe about Pender's phone conversation. "Pender has a motive. He's the one who's broke, not Leona." He opened the sack and handed Joe the ski mask. "I bought this in his shop. What's more, there was a white one with a blue lightning bolt on the table. They're both similar in style to the ones the thieves were wearing. And guess who came in just as I was leaving? Craig Thompson."

"What are we waiting for?" Joe said. "Let's get this evidence to Meyers and tell him about the connection between Pender and Thompson."

Frank and Joe hurried into the rec hall and went straight to Meyers's office. They told Meyers what they had learned and gave him the ski mask. Meyers looked interested but skeptical. "Too bad being broke isn't a crime. We'll need more evidence than this ski mask to make an arrest."

"We'll keep working on it," Joe said, and turned toward the door.

As the boys stepped outside, Chet came running over to them. "Didn't you say it was a white minivan that tried to run you down?" he asked.

"Why?" Frank wanted to know.

"Because there's a white minivan in the parking lot," Chet explained breathlessly. "Come on!"

Frank, Joe, and Chet all rushed out of the rec hall and toward the parking lot. As soon as they got there, Frank pointed out to Joe a white minivan backing out of a parking space. Joe led the race to their own van, climbing behind the wheel. Frank and Chet were right behind.

Frank scrambled into the front seat as Joe pulled onto the street after the van. "He's spotted us," Frank said. "Stick with him."

The minivan turned right, picked up speed, and roared around the curve at the base of Bradford's hill. Joe took the curve as fast as he could.

That's when Frank and Joe found themselves staring straight into the grille of an approaching car.

11 Thin Ice

Frantically, Joe Hardy swerved to avoid the head-on collision. He cut the wheel, first one way, then the other. He tapped the gas pedal, hoping to get some traction to the wheels—at least enough to control the slide. Nothing did any good.

In the backseat, Chet screamed, "Do something, Joe! We're going to crash!"

"Hold on, Chet!" Frank shouted. "Brace yourself!"

Then, with a bone-jarring, neck-wrenching jolt, the van dove into a ditch and abruptly stopped. Joe held his breath. There was absolute silence, then Chet yelled out, "We're okay, we made it! I can't believe we're actually okay."

"That was close," Frank agreed. "But there goes the white minivan."

Joe looked up just in time to see the minivan turn off onto a side road and drive out of sight. He opened the door, jumped to the ground, and ran around to the front of the van. Both front tires were in the ditch.

He dropped to his knees and looked under the van. "We can forget catching up to him. Our van's sitting on its axle. We'll need a tow truck."

"I'll walk back to the park and call the garage," Frank said.

After Frank left, Chet got out of the van and stood shivering and rubbing his hands together. "I vote for waiting inside," he said to Joe. He opened the door and climbed in the back, while Joe sat behind the steering wheel.

As soon as they got settled, Joe nodded toward the road the minivan had turned onto. "What's down there?"

"I don't know," Chet said. "After Frank gets back here with the tow truck, we can find out."

Chet lifted a blanket and looked under it. "Don't suppose you've got any of your aunt's cookies in here?"

Joe grinned. "Sorry, bud. You're out of luck."

The tow truck arrived thirty minutes later and pulled the van out of the ditch. Joe started the engine, then checked the lights and brakes. "Everything works," he said. "We're in business."

After the tow-truck driver left, Joe continued driving down the road. "Now, let's see where that guy went." He turned onto the side road a few moments later and saw that it was barely wide enough for two cars to pass. Along the road's edge, a thick stubble of dead weeds and bushes jutted through the dirty slush left by a snowplow. On his left, Joe saw smoke rising from the chimney of a run-down house, then there was nothing but woods. The crumbling wall surrounding the Bradford estate was on his right.

A minute or two later, Frank spotted a break in the wall. "Must be the back entrance," he said, pointing to an overgrown driveway. The gate was secured by a heavy chain and padlock. "Hold on, Joe," Frank said, leaning forward. "Check it out. There's fresh car tracks in the driveway. They might belong to the minivan."

Joe pulled off the road and parked. Chet stayed inside when the Hardys got out and walked to the foot of the driveway.

"There are a lot of tracks here," Joe said. "Some of them are fresh, and some are a couple of days old, judging by the snow in them." He noticed that someone had cut some dead shrubbery and piled it neatly to one side. He nodded toward the chain and padlock. "They look new, too. What do you think?"

Frank pursed his lips. "Judging from the shrubbery, I'd guess it must be the estate's caretaker. He must have made the tracks."

"You're probably right," Joe agreed. "There's

no way to prove it was our guy in the minivan who was here." He kicked the snow. "I just wish we hadn't had that accident. We could have learned so much more if we'd been able to follow him."

The Hardys returned to the van, climbed in, and continued along the road. It came to a T at the road north of the park, across from the new mall. "So much for finding the white minivan," Frank said. "He could be anywhere."

"While we're here, we might as well eat an early dinner," Chet said. "That new burger place has terrific fries."

"He's right," Frank said. "We've got time before the speed-skating event, don't we?"

In all the excitement, Joe had almost forgotten about the competition. He began to get psyched and realized he was starving. "Walk-in or drive-through?" he asked.

"Drive-through," both Frank and Chet agreed.

It was dark by the time the boys finished eating. Joe looked at his watch and saw it was already five-thirty. The skating competition started at six. "We'd better get going," Joe said. "The races start in half an hour. I don't want to be late. Craig Thompson might have the mistaken idea that he's got the race sewn up."

They drove to the park, got their skates from the back of the van, and made their way to the lake. There, a crowd had already gathered for the speed-skating events. Joe spotted Craig Thompson sitting on the far end of the contestants' bench. His pals were in the stands behind him.

Joe and Frank found seats on the opposite end of the bench from Thompson and put on their skates. Chet spotted his parents in the stands and went to sit with them. A few minutes later, the race officials called the sprinters onto the ice and motioned for them to take their places behind the starting line. Unlike the Olympics, where skaters raced the clock, this thousand-meter was a free-for-all. Everyone skated at once. Whoever crossed the finish line first was the winner.

Joe looked at Craig Thompson, who was five spaces to his left. Thompson glared at him, then turned back to watch the official starter. Joe glanced at Frank, three spaces away, and smiled when his brother gave him the thumbs-up sign. Joe held his breath in excitement. Whatever it took, he'd beat Thompson.

Suddenly, the starting gun sounded.

It caught Joe off guard. He dug the toe of his skate into the ice and pushed off. But that one second's hesitation meant he was late leaving the starting line.

Thompson already had a ten-yard lead!

Joe dug in and planted his left arm on his back in the classic racing stance. His powerful glide began eating into Craig's lead. At the halfway point, the distance between them was still five yards. The first of two turns was coming up.

If he was going to win the race, he had to make his move! Both of Joe's arms were swinging now, adding momentum to each glide.

He went into the turn flat-out. The edges of his blades cut a razor-thin line in the ice. One wrong move and he'd be down.

Craig was only three yards ahead when Joe came out of the turn. As they went into the next turn, only two yards separated them. The muscles in Joe's thighs felt as though they were on fire, his feet like lead as one foot crossed in front of the other. Five strides later, Joe was out of the turn, digging for the home stretch. The crowd roared.

Out of the corner of his eye, Joe saw Craig's back. Then he was beside him, matching Thompson glide for glide. The finish line was only yards away.

The crowd was on their feet cheering. Every muscle in Joe's body strained for more speed.

He gained three inches, then six. A sudden burst of speed put him a whole two feet ahead of Thompson as they crossed the finish line.

"All right!" came a cry. Frank Hardy rushed over to congratulate Joe. Thompson brushed by on his way back to the bench. "You got lucky this time, Hardy," Thompson said.

Craig Thompson turned out to be wrong. For the rest of the night, Frank and Joe proved they were the better skaters. Joe won the fifteen-hundred-meter sprint and Frank won the three-thousand-meter race. When it was all over, Thompson glared at Joe and stomped away from the lake. Frank tucked his gift certificate in his pocket and scanned the crowd.

"Who are you looking for?" Joe asked.

"David Kennedy," Frank answered. "Didn't he say he'd be here to watch?"

"Hey, that's right," Joe said. "Too bad. He missed out on some great skating."

"Way to go," Chet said, coming over to give both Hardys a congratulatory handshake. Then he let out a long yawn. "Well, I'm ready to call it a night. I'm beat!"

Joe shook his head and grinned. "How do you like this guy? We've been on the ice all night, and he's the one who's tired."

"Can we give you a ride?" Frank asked.

"No, thanks. I'll go home with my folks. Catch you guys tomorrow," Chet said.

The speed skating was the last event of the night. The crowd drifted off, heading toward the park exits. Joe and Frank took off their skates, then made their way along the crowded footpath. Frank was putting their skates in the van when Joe grabbed him by the jacket.

"Hey, Frank. Check it out. It's the white van!"

As Frank turned to look, the driver got out of the minivan, which was parked across the lot. Just then a family of four passed by, blocking both

Hardys' view. Frank craned his neck and caught a glimpse of the man heading into the park. He had a large build and was wearing tan pants.

"Get the license number of the van," Frank said. "I'll follow him."

Frank raced off after the guy, while Joe went for the license-plate number. But Frank lost sight of the guy among the people leaving the park. Frank was standing in front of the rec hall, scanning the crowd, when Joe hurried to his side.

"I got the license number," Joe said. "Where's the guy?"

"I don't know," Frank said, searching the crowd. "I lost him as soon as I got inside the park. He just disappeared."

"He could be anywhere," Joe said. "The park's a big place."

"Let's wait at the bridge," Frank said. "He's got to cross it to get back to the minivan."

"Good idea. Let's go," Joe said.

Ten minutes or so after they reached the bridge, hardly anyone was left in the park. "Do you think we missed him?" Joe asked.

"I'll check the parking lot," Frank said. "Be back in a minute."

When Frank reached the parking lot, only a few cars remained. Relieved to see that the minivan was one of them, he turned and headed back toward the bridge. But as he drew near, Frank's stomach clenched. His brother was struggling with two men wearing ski masks in the middle of the bridge!

Joe's hand shot out and delivered a karate chop to the taller man's throat. The shorter man wrapped his arms around Joe from behind.

Frank rushed to Joe's aid, taking down the shorter man with a flying tackle. As Frank scrambled to his feet, he saw Joe hit the taller man in the solar plexus. The man bent double as the air rushed from his lungs.

Just when it looked as if the boys were going to hold their own, the shorter man lunged at Joe. His weight slammed Joe into the railing of the bridge. With a loud snap, the old wood splintered.

Joe appeared to hang in midair for a moment. Then, with an ear-splitting scream, he dropped from sight.

12 Kidnapped!

Frank rushed to the railing. Joe lay spread-eagle on the frozen stream below. His eyes were open, but he looked as if the wind had been knocked out of him. The ice cracked beneath Joe, and with a loud groaning noise, it began to sag. Frank's chest tightened in helpless terror as he watched water pour through the crack.

Then the ice broke—and Joe plunged into the freezing water.

"Joe!" Frank shouted. "I'll be right there!"

"Let's get out of here," one of the attackers said.

Frank heard the attackers' retreating footsteps as Joe shot to the surface. Frank watched as his brother grabbed the edge of the ice and tried to pull himself out. Frantically, Frank ran along the bridge and vaulted the railing. He slid down the sloping creek bank and began racing along the stream toward his brother.

"Hang on!" Frank urged Joe, who was barely managing to keep his head above water.

Frank glanced around, hoping to spot a stick or a fallen limb—anything that would reach from the creek bank to the center of the stream, where Joe's head was bobbing.

"Hurry," Joe shouted. "I can't stay afloat much longer."

Frank spotted a tree branch about as thick as a baseball bat sticking out of the snow. He yanked it free and held it toward Joe. The icy water was sapping Joe's strength by the minute. He could barely hold on to the limb. His hands clutched the branch in desperation.

Just as Frank started to pull Joe toward the shore, the aged limb snapped in half.

Joe again plunged under the water. Frank held his breath in fear for a long moment until he saw Joe resurface.

Frank knew his brother was running out of time. He had to do something fast.

He grabbed a rock about the size of his fist, tied it into a ball at the end of his neck scarf, and stepped onto the ice. He heard the ice groan and felt it give beneath his feet.

Quickly, he dropped to his hands and knees, then stretched out on his stomach, distributing his weight more evenly. Slowly, he began inching his way toward Joe.

As Frank reached the gaping hole, he felt the ice beneath him sag. With his head and shoulders hanging over the icy water, Frank tossed the rock-weighted end of the scarf toward Joe.

Joe grabbed for it but missed.

Quickly, Frank pulled the scarf to him and tried again.

This time, Joe caught the scarf and held on.

Frank wrapped the scarf around his wrist and began backing up. In relief, he watched as Joe squirmed onto the sagging ice and slowly, foot by foot, inched toward the shore.

Finally, Frank felt firm ground under his feet. He crouched down and, hand over hand, began pulling Joe toward the bank.

Joe was only a couple of feet away when the ice beneath him exploded. "Frank!" Joe cried, plunging once again into the icy stream.

"Joe!" In desperation, Frank reached out and barely managed to grab a handful of Joe's jacket.

By the time Frank pulled his brother's head above the water, Joe's lips were blue and his teeth were chattering. "Fre . . . fre . . . freezing," Joe said.

Frank knew he should report the attack. He also knew Joe was suffering from hypothermia. If he didn't get Joe warm in a hurry, he would die. With one arm around his brother, Frank helped

110

him to the van. "Get out of those wet clothes, quick," Frank said, taking off his down jacket and handing it to Joe. "Put this on."

Joe began stripping out of his wet clothes. Frank got inside, started the engine, and cranked the heater as high as it would go. Joe settled into the passenger seat while Frank headed them both for home.

Frank knew that Joe's blood was probably chilled and that he had to be warmed from the inside out. "You're going to be all right," Frank assured his brother. "We'll get you into a hot bath. You'll be fine."

"You saved my life," Joe managed to say. "Another minute in that water—"

"And you'd have been a contestant in the Polar Bear Club," Frank said, trying to make a joke. Now that they were on their way home, and Frank knew Joe would soon get indoors and warm, he could let himself think about how close a call they'd really had.

At home, Aunt Gertrude met them at the door, her eyes wide with excitement. "You'll never believe what happened!" At the sight of Joe, in just his shorts and the down jacket, her mouth dropped open. "What on earth?"

"Joe fell into the river," Frank explained. By now, Joe was shivering uncontrollably. "We've got to raise his body temperature."

"Go upstairs and get a thick blanket," Aunt Gertrude said.

When Frank came back downstairs, Joe sat at the table. His skin looked gray. His feet were soaking in a pan of hot water. Chicken broth was heating on the stove. Joe wrapped the blanket around himself. As soon as the broth was hot, Aunt Gertrude poured a mug and handed it to Joe.

"I just have one question for you boys," Aunt Gertrude said. "Where were the security guards while all this was going on?"

"Who knows," Frank said. "Judging from their build, I'd say the two guys who attacked Joe could very well be our robbers. Too bad no one was around to stop them."

"You didn't get a look at their faces?" Aunt Gertrude asked.

"I got something almost as good," Joe said. "The license number of the minivan."

"That's right!" Frank said. In all the excitement, he had completely forgotten that Joe had taken down the number of the van. "Let me have it. I'll call Con Riley and get him to run it through the computer."

Frank quickly got in touch with Con Riley. The police officer was glad to run a check on the van. Just before he hung up, Con Riley asked Frank if his aunt Gertrude was all right. "I think so," Frank said. "Why?"

"You might want to ask her about what happened at the park this afternoon," Riley told him. With that, Con said a quick goodbye. "I'll call you when we get a report on the van."

When Frank returned to the kitchen table, he shot his aunt a puzzled look. "Officer Riley asked if you were all right, Aunt Gertrude. What happened?"

"You'll never believe it," she said. "Someone tried to rob my booth."

Joe's mouth dropped open. Frank's eyes widened. "At gunpoint?" he asked.

Aunt Gertrude had a smug look on her face. "Yes, but he didn't get one red cent. I was ready for him. Since the robberies, I decided it was best to be prepared. I've been taking one of your old hockey sticks to the booth with me."

"Hockey stick?" Joe grinned. "You didn't?"

"Oh, yes I did," she said. "When that creep waved his gun in my face, I hit him with the stick. Knocked the gun right out of his hand. Then I started yelling for help, and he ran off—empty-handed, I might add."

Frank leaned forward. "Without the gun?"

"Of course," she said. "Dan Meyers was on the scene in a flash. He took charge of the gun."

"Can you describe the thief?" Joe asked.

"I didn't see his face because he wore a dark ski mask with stars on it, but he was tall and thin," she said. "He wore a white jacket with a stripe on the sleeves. Oh, yes. I caught a flash of gold, maybe a ring, but I can't be sure."

"That means he wasn't wearing gloves. Now we're getting somewhere," Frank said.

"Right," Joe said. "The gun will have his fingerprints on it."

"I didn't hear anyone talking about it at the park," Frank said. "When did this happen?"

"Early evening," Gertrude said. "Right around the time the skating ended. I know because we could hear the cheering at the booths."

"Looks like the guy in the minivan was the getaway driver," Frank said. "When the one who tried to rob you didn't show up, he went to look for him. Apparently, they decided to lay low until the crowd thinned out."

"That makes sense," Joe said. "When they spotted me on the bridge, they probably thought I knew about the robbery and was looking for them."

"Well, we can talk about it some more tomorrow," Aunt Gertrude said. "I know it's long past my bedtime. And I'm sure Joe is ready to get under some nice warm covers."

"You bet I am," Joe said. "This has been one long day."

"That's right," Frank said. "And tomorrow we've got to keep working on the case. What's the expression? Get right back on the ice?"

"Ice." Joe groaned, standing up with the blanket around his shoulders. "Promise me, Frank—you won't use that word around me again. Ever."

When Frank and Joe came downstairs the next morning, Aunt Gertrude had breakfast waiting for them. "I've got good news and bad news," she said. "Officer Riley called. The license plate was stolen. It's not going to help."

"I'm not surprised," Frank said. "What's the good news?"

"I talked to Ron Smithson, the festival director. It looks as though Kennedy's performance is going to be a sellout. If it is, the festival will raise the fifty thousand, despite the robberies."

"That is good news," Joe agreed, sipping his juice.

Frank nodded. "Speaking of Kennedy, we should stop by his hotel and find out where he was last night. I'm surprised he missed the skating event."

"Me, too," Joe said. "And after hanging around with us so much, he just sort of disappeared."

When the boys stepped outside the air was so crisp and clear that Frank felt as though he could see for a thousand miles. The snow underfoot was crunchy and sparkled in the thin winter sunlight. Frank backed the van out of the driveway. They arrived at Kennedy's hotel twenty minutes later and rode the elevator up to the third floor. As they stepped into the hall, they saw Ivan Petrovich insert a card into a door lock.

"Good morning, Mr. Petrovich," Joe said.

Obviously startled, Ivan turned. He took one look at the boys and frowned. "David isn't with you?" he asked.

"With us?" Frank echoed, looking at Joe. "No. Why?"

Frank saw a look of panic in Ivan's eyes as he fumbled with the card. "David didn't show up for practice this morning," he said. "I got this pass key to his room at the front desk."

Joe and Frank followed him through the doorway. One look at the mess of a room was enough to tell Frank there had been a struggle—and that David Kennedy was gone.

13 Clue from the Past

One chair lay on its side, the other was upside down. The lamp had been knocked off the table. The shade was bent, the base shattered. The drapes hung halfway off the rod, as if someone had grabbed hold and hung on for dear life.

Joe looked at Frank. The older Hardy shook his head. "This is bad," Frank said. "I'll ask down at the front desk if anyone has seen him."

"David once trashed his room," Ivan said. "He was mad about something a reporter wrote."

"This room wasn't trashed," Joe said. "There's been a struggle."

"A struggle?" Ivan repeated. "Then David could be . . ."

"In very serious trouble," Joe said, finishing the

thought. "Unless I'm wrong, it looks as if he's been kidnapped."

Frank was panting for breath when he ran back into the room five minutes later. "No one's seen him. I'm going to call the police." Frank turned to Petrovich. "Can I use the phone in your room? There may be fingerprints on the one in here."

"Of course," Petrovich said. "I'll come with you."

"I'll stand guard here to make sure no one touches anything," Joe said.

While Frank and Ivan were gone, Joe wandered around the room, looking for clues, but he didn't discover more than what had first met the eye: David Kennedy had obviously fought hard and lost.

Frank came back a few minutes later, alone. "The police are on their way."

"Where's Petrovich?" Joe asked.

"He's calling Kennedy's folks," Frank said.

"What happened here, Frank?" Joe wondered aloud. "Why Kennedy?"

Frank frowned. "I don't know. Is there some connection here to the robberies? And if so, what? Is this another way for the thieves to get money fast?"

"We'll have to wait and see if there's a ransom note," Joe said. "Unless . . ." Something his aunt Gertrude had said was nagging at him. "Kennedy's performance was the big draw to end the festival. The hospital was going to make its fifty thousand with the money from the tickets sold. But with David gone—"

"There won't be any performance," Frank put in.

"Exactly." Quickly, Joe felt the pieces fitting together. "Maybe the gunshot at the sleigh ride was an attempt to injure David so he couldn't skate. When that didn't work, they kidnapped him. With David missing, the hospital won't get its money. So who has the most to gain here?"

"The Bradford heirs," Frank said.

"Bingo!" Joe exclaimed. "That's been the motive all along. Whoever is heir to the Bradford fortune wants the festival to fail. They must have gone for Kennedy when they realized that the robberies weren't doing the job. Find the Bradford heir, and you've got the culprit, right?"

"Right," Frank agreed.

Before either Hardy could say anything more, Officer Riley walked through the door. "I was only a couple of blocks away when the call came over the radio," Con Riley explained. "What's this about David Kennedy being kidnapped?"

Frank and Joe were telling Riley about finding the mess in the room when Petrovich returned. They had barely finished when Police Chief Collig bustled in. Quickly, the Hardys and Riley brought Collig up to date.

"When was the last time you saw Kennedy?" Collig asked Petrovich.

"Last night, right after dinner," Petrovich answered. "We had room service bring something up. He planned to go the park afterward and watch the speed-skating events. When we finished eating, I returned to my room. I haven't seen him since."

"He wasn't at the park," Frank said. "When the events were over, I looked for him."

Chief Collig let out a long breath. "It looks like a kidnapping. I'm going to call in the FBI." He then turned to Officer Riley. "Get the crime-scene crew in here. I want this place dusted for prints. And call for some backup. Have them search every room in the hotel."

"Frank and I think whoever did this is behind the robberies," Joe put in. "We think the Bradford heir—"

Chief Collig turned and pointed at the Hardys. "Keep out of this. It's a police matter. If there's any detective work to be done, I'll do it. Now get out of here, both of you."

Frank could tell the chief meant business, so he hustled out of the room, pushing Joe ahead of him.

Officer Riley followed the boys into the hall. "Thought you'd want to know," he said, his voice barely above a whisper. "There weren't any prints on the gun used in the attempted robbery of your aunt's booth." Riley glanced back at the hotel room. "Keep up the good work," he added. "But watch out for Collig."

As soon as Officer Riley walked away, Joe turned to Frank. "Are we going to stay out of Kennedy's kidnapping, like the chief said?"

"What do you think?" Frank said.

Joe's face relaxed into a smile. "I think Con Riley knows us too well for that. Why do you think he told us to keep up the good work?" Joe asked as they headed toward the elevator. "So where do we start? How are we going to find out who was supposed to inherit Bradford's millions? Do you think it's Roger Pender?"

"Could be," said Frank. "He's new to Bayport, and we don't know much about him. And from the looks of his store, he sure could use the money." Frank thought for a moment. "I think our best trail right now is David himself. First of all, he could be in real danger. Second, if we find him, we'll find our culprit, right?"

"Good thinking," Joe said. The elevator stopped on the first floor. When the doors opened, Joe nodded toward the restaurant. "I didn't see any dirty dishes in Kennedy's room. Let's start in there and see if we can find out who delivered his dinner. They might have seen something."

When they walked into the restaurant, Joe approached the hostess. "Miss, are the room-service orders delivered from the restaurant?"

121

The smile faded from her face. "Don't tell me they mixed up an order again?"

"Our dinner was fine," Joe said. "We'd like the name of the man who delivered it so we can tell his supervisor what a terrific job he did."

Frank had to smile. Joe could always charm his way through any situation.

She reached under the counter and pulled out a schedule. "Let's see. Howie Kaiser was working last night."

The boys thanked her and left. Frank stopped at the pay phone in the lobby. He opened the phone book to *K* and ran his finger down the listings. "Howie Kaiser. Hey, there's a Howard Kaiser at 2319 Maple Street."

"What are we waiting for?" Joe said.

When they knocked at the door of that address ten minutes later, it was answered by a dark-haired man in his early twenties.

"We're looking for Howie Kaiser, a waiter at the Bayport Hotel," Frank said.

"That's me," he answered. "What's up?"

Frank and Joe showed him their badges and explained they were working with the festival security force. "There's been some trouble involving David Kennedy," Frank said. "When you took his dinner to his room, did you see anyone hanging around in the hallways?"

Kaiser shook his head. "No, man. What happened? Did someone break into his room?"

122

"Yes," Joe said. "Did you see anyone suspicious in the elevator or the lobby?"

Again, Kaiser shook his head. "I wish I could help you guys. I just didn't see a thing." Frank and Joe were headed back down the walk, when Kaiser called them back. "Wait a minute," he said. "Come to think of it, I did see two men when I picked up Kennedy's tray. They came out of the stairwell as I was getting on the elevator."

Joe hoped this was the break they were looking for. "Can you describe them?" he asked.

Kaiser shook his head. "One was tall and thin. The other was shorter, a little huskier. I got the feeling they were repairmen."

"What gave you that idea?" Frank asked.

"They were dressed alike in tan outfits. That's all I can tell you. My shift was over, and I was in a hurry to get home to watch the game. Afraid I didn't pay much attention."

"Thanks again," Frank said.

As soon as the Hardys were back in the van, Joe announced to Frank, "Kaiser's description sounds exactly like the two guys who threw me in the river. So where do we find them?"

"I don't know," Frank said in frustration.

"And another thing," Joe said. "What connection do they have to Bradford's heir? Did the heir hire them?"

Frank held up his hands. "Time out! One question at a time. We've got to have a strategy here, Joe. You're piling on the problems like there's no tomorrow."

"You're right." Joe ran his hand through his hair and thought. "We agree that the Bradford heir is the best lead, right?"

"Right."

"So let's find out who he—or she—is," Joe said, putting the van into gear.

"Where are we going?" Frank asked.

"The library, of course," Joe said with a smile.

It was snowing heavily when Joe stopped in front of the library. The Hardys entered the stone building and made their way to the basement, where copies of the *Bayport Times* were stored on microfilm. Frank and Joe started with the year Bradford died and began working their way backward through the society pages of the old newspapers.

They had covered twenty years before they found what they were looking for. "Check it out," Joe said, calling Frank's attention to an article in the paper about a summer social in the park, including pictures. In one of them, Louis Bradford was seated in the center of several people. His daughter, Dolores, stood behind him. She was looking at the man at her side.

Joe read aloud from the caption, "'Louis Bradford, his daughter, Dolores, and son-in-law, Benjamin Meyers.'"

"You don't think?" Frank whispered.

"Oh, yes, I do," Joe said, staring at the photograph. "Unless I'm very wrong, Dan Meyers is Louis Bradford's heir."

14 Confrontation

"Remember what Kennedy said about an optical illusion?" Joe said. "That when he was out of costume, people didn't recognize him?"

"I guess." Frank tried to follow what Joe was saying. "What's the significance?"

"Think about it, Frank." Joe leaned back in his seat. "If Meyers is behind the robberies, then who are the two guys in tan pants? The ones Kaiser said he thought were wearing uniforms."

Suddenly, it dawned on Frank exactly where Joe was leading. "Adams and Jones," Frank whispered under his breath.

"We were looking for thieves, not security guards," Joe reasoned. "That's why we never connected them to the robberies. When it came time to pull off the robberies, Jones and Adams simply changed their jackets. No one recognized them out of costume. As for the tan pants, their uniforms are khaki, plus they fit the description of the robbers—Jones is big and burly, and Adams is tall and thin."

"And they both carry guns," Frank added.

"The gun!" Joe said loudly. Patrons in the library turned around to stare, so Joe lowered his voice. "Aunt Gertrude said the thief didn't wear gloves. There should have been prints on that gun. Con Riley said none were found."

"But Meyers was in charge of the investigation," Frank said. "Obviously, he wiped the prints off the gun." He let out a low whistle. "Smithson played right into Meyers's hands when he insisted we work on the case. We've been reporting every move we made directly to Meyers. No wonder we couldn't come up with any real leads! Meyers has been one step ahead of us all the way."

"And no wonder Craig Thompson didn't fit into the puzzle. Thompson had nothing to do with the robberies. He's just an obnoxious little punk, that's all." Joe got out of his chair and said, "Well, what are we waiting for? Let's go tell Chief Collig."

"Hold on a minute," Frank said, pulling Joe back into his seat. "He didn't listen to us before," Frank pointed out, "and I don't think the FBI will either. Not without proof." He shook his head slowly and bit on his lower lip. "Nope, we're on

127

our own on this one, Joe. We'll have to nail Meyers ourselves."

"Got a plan?" Joe asked.

"Do you?" Frank shot back.

Joe's brow furrowed. "Maybe. Just maybe. But we're going to need some help."

"From Chet?" Frank asked.

"Would you believe Aunt Gertrude?" Joe said with a smile. "Isn't it about time she joined the Hardys in crimefighting? It's a family tradition, after all."

From the library, Frank called home to Aunt Gertrude and explained to her what they needed to know. "Call Bayport Security Company and find out all you can about Adams, Jones, and Meyers," Frank said. "Meanwhile, Joe and I are going to contact Dad to get the other information we need. We have to be sure that Dan Meyers is related to Louis Bradford—and that he's the only living Bradford heir."

"Then what?" Aunt Gertrude asked tentatively. "I'm new to this, Frank. You're going to have to fill me in."

Frank laughed. "You're doing just fine. Joe and I are going to head straight to the park. We've got to keep an eye on Meyers. David Kennedy could be in danger, and we'll have to hope that Meyers leads us to him."

Aunt Gertrude drew in a sharp breath. "Oh, it's

128

just awful how all this has turned out," she said. "I hope nothing's happened to that nice boy."

"Me, too," Frank said. "Me, too." With that, Frank made arrangements for Aunt Gertrude to meet them in the rec hall—as soon as possible.

On the way over to the park, Joe spotted a store with a fax advertisement in the window. He and Frank went inside and faxed their father at his hotel in New York, asking him to check the Bureau of Vital Statistics for a marriage license between Benjamin Meyers and Dolores Bradford. He also asked him to check birth certificates and see if they had any children or grandchildren.

"Okay," Frank said as they were leaving the store. "Ready to play cat and mouse?"

"Are you kidding? I can't wait to nail Meyers," Joe said. "Let's just hope it doesn't take too long for him to tip his hand."

By the time Frank and Joe reached the park, snowflakes as big as quarters swirled through the air, and they could only see ten feet ahead. Joe parked the van in the lot. On the way to the rec hall, the Hardys ran into Chet. They quickly briefed Chet on what they'd learned about Dan Meyers. When Chet heard that David Kennedy was missing, his eyes went wide.

"You're kidding!" he said. "And you think Jones and Adams and Meyers did it? Wow!"

"We're going to stake out Meyers now," Joe

said. "And hope he leads us to Kennedy. Want to come?"

Chet's eyes flickered. "I wish I could, but I'm heading the parade tonight," he said. "After I eat lunch, I've got to get over to Oak Street. That's where the parade is lining up. It's going to circle downtown and end up back at the park."

"Too bad," Joe said. "You're going to miss all the excitement."

"I know," Chet said glumly. "I wish I hadn't promised to be in the float. But you know how Leona Turner is. If I let her down—"

"Say no more," Frank said. "You'd better go."

After Chet had left, Frank and Joe headed into the rec hall. They went directly to Meyers's office, only to find the entire security force was shut down. A sign on the door read Out to Lunch. Back in Five.

"Yeah, right," Frank said, kicking the door in frustration. "I don't know about you, but I'd say Meyers has taken off—with no forwarding address."

"What are we going to do?" Joe asked. "We're facing the biggest dead end of the case here, Frank."

"Thanks for pointing that out to me, Joe," Frank said. "I could never have figured that out myself."

"Cool your jets, Frank," Joe said. "I want to catch Meyers as much as you. Come on, let's grab a hot dog while we wait for Aunt Gertrude to show up. Maybe she'll have some news."

"We could use it right now," Frank agreed.

In the rec hall, the boys each bought a hot dog and some chips. A few minutes later, when Aunt Gertrude came into the hall, Frank waved and rushed over to greet her.

"Sorry I'm late," she said breathlessly. "Since the media broadcast the fact that Kennedy is missing, the phone's been ringing off the hook with calls from people who want their money back. If Kennedy doesn't skate, the festival will never raise enough money. And his exhibition is scheduled only hours from now. What are we going to do?"

"Get Meyers," Frank said. "Did the security agency cooperate?"

Aunt Gertrude nodded. "Turns out the man I was talking to once worked with your dad on a case. Get this. Meyers has only been with the agency six months. Before that, he was head of security for a large warehousing firm in New York. When Meyers learned the agency had been hired for Bayport's festival, he asked to be placed in charge but was turned down."

"Then why is he here?" Joe asked.

"They're working shorthanded," Aunt Gertrude said. "Half their men are out with a flu bug. The man that was assigned as head of security for the festival was the victim of a hit-and-run two days before the festival was due to open. He's in the hospital."

"Let me guess," Frank said. "Meyers stepped forward and volunteered to take his place."

"Exactly," Aunt Gertrude said. "Do you think he was responsible for the hit-and-run?"

"It's possible," Frank said. "I wouldn't put anything past the guy."

"Well, even though most of the guards have been with the firm a long time, Meyers got the job because he was the only one left with management experience," Aunt Gertrude said. "By the way—Jones and Adams were last-minute replacements. They were hired by Meyers."

"We still don't have enough evidence to take to the FBI," Frank said. "Not until we get a full report from our fax to Dad."

"Well, we can't just sit around and do nothing either," Joe said. "These guys are playing rough, and they're getting desperate. They might decide to get rid of Kennedy any minute—permanently."

"Right," Frank said. He turned to his aunt expectantly. "Meyers isn't in his office. Did you get a home address for him or Adams and Jones?"

"Right here," Aunt Gertrude said, and handed him a slip of paper.

In relief, Frank looked at the paper. "All three of them live in the same apartment complex. It's close to the library, about six blocks from here."

"That could be where they're holding Kennedy," Joe said. "Let's see what their neighbors can tell us."

"I'll go home and wait for Fenton's fax," Aunt Gertrude said.

The clouds were breaking up as Joe, Frank, and Aunt Gertrude made their way to the parking lot. As soon as Aunt Gertrude backed out of her parking slot, the boys climbed in their van and headed toward Meyers's place. At the corner of Oak Street, where the parade would begin its route, they had to wait for two floats to cross. As soon as the road was clear, Joe stepped on the gas. They reached the apartment complex ten minutes later.

"Meyers is in building C," Frank said. "I'll check it out. You head over to building B and see what you can find out. Let's meet back here in half an hour. If one of us is missing after that, call Con and get backup."

"Got it," Joe said.

Frank started with Meyers's apartment. There was no answer at the second-floor unit. He went from door to door, but no one remembered seeing a boy answering Kennedy's description. Half an hour later, Frank returned to the van. Joe was waiting for him, a dejected look on his face.

"I struck out," Joe said.

"Me, too," Frank said. "So what do we do now? We still don't have a clue as to where Meyers is holding David."

133

"There's a phone booth on the corner," Joe pointed out. "Let's call home and see if Dad answered our fax."

Aunt Gertrude answered the phone on the second ring. She sounded excited. "The answer to your fax is coming in now, Frank," she said. "It's all here, in black and white. Dolores and Benjamin Meyers had one child, a son named Richard. Shortly after Richard's son, Daniel, was born, Richard died in an automobile accident. Dolores died of old age six months ago, a year after her husband, Benjamin, passed away. Daniel Louis Meyers is Bradford's great-grandson and only living heir."

"That's the proof we need," Frank said. "I just hope it's not too late to save Kennedy."

He hung up and told Joe the news.

"That's great," Joe said. "Let's get the fax and take it to police headquarters. The FBI and Chief Collig will have to believe us now."

"Let's hope so," Frank said as they climbed in the van. "Without Kennedy, and without Meyers, we don't have conclusive proof."

"True," Joe said. "But everything is falling into place. The way I see it, the first robbery was a scam. I bet all three of them—Meyers, Adams, and Jones—cooked up the plan ahead of time. After ripping off the booth, Adams met Jones somewhere in the park and passed the money to

134

him. When Chet happened along and picked up the ski mask, Adams and Jones decided to make him the scapegoat."

"It fits," Frank agreed. "But they didn't count on Chet having an alibi—us. Once Meyers saw that the first robbery wasn't going to do the trick, he planned another. He must have had Jones wear a maroon jacket so it'd look like Chet did it."

"Do you think Jones ditched the ski mask and maroon jacket in the Dumpster so we'd think either Leona or Pender was guilty?" Joe asked.

"Probably," Frank said. "Which wasn't such a bad move. It almost worked."

As they turned the corner, Frank spotted the white minivan parked in front of a grocery store halfway down the block. Frank let out a low whistle. "There's our man," he said. He unhooked his seat belt and had his hand on the door. "Drop me off," he said. "We don't want to lose the van again. It could lead us to Kennedy. You get to a phone and call the police. And try to keep the van in sight," Frank pleaded. "I don't want to get stranded out here."

"Roger," Joe said. "I'm just going over there." He pointed to a pay phone up the street. "I won't lose you, don't worry." With that, Joe pulled to a stop long enough for Frank to hop out. Then, with a squeal of tires, he sped off.

Frank hurried over to the white minivan. He

135

was scanning the shoppers on the sidewalk when he felt a huge pair of arms wrap him in a bear hug from behind.

"Nice to see you, Frank," came a voice.

Frank turned around and found himself staring straight at Trevor Jones.

And then, before Frank could break free, the side door of the white van flew open. Jones shoved him inside. Frank went sprawling on his face, right at Dan Meyers's feet.

15 The Front Row

Frank tried to get up, but Meyers pulled a gun. He put his foot on Frank's neck, keeping him pinned to the floorboard. "Stay put, Frank," Meyers said. "We're going for a little ride."

"Where are you holding Kennedy?" Frank asked.

"You'll see soon enough," Meyers said, then he turned to Jones, who was driving. "Step on it. I want to have this wrapped up before the parade ends."

From his position on the floor, Frank couldn't tell where they were going. He tried to figure it out by counting right and left turns. It seemed to him they might be headed toward the park, which couldn't be right, since there were too many people there to make it a safe place to hide David Kennedy.

A few minutes later, the van stopped. Jones left the engine running and got out. Frank heard the screech of metal, then Jones got back in and put the van in gear. When it started up a steep hill, Frank knew where they were. The van stopped again a moment later. Jones came around and opened the door. "Okay, Hardy. End of the line," he said.

Meyers removed his foot from Frank's neck. "Move it. I'm in a hurry," he said.

Frank climbed out of the van and looked at the peeling paint on the Bradford mansion. His hunch was correct.

Jones poked his gun barrel in Frank's ribs and prodded him toward the door. When Frank stepped inside, it took his eyes a moment to adjust to the dimness. He was in a large center hall. The cold air smelled moldy. Huge spiderwebs hung in the corners of the high ceilings, collecting dust.

Then he saw Adams standing guard over David Kennedy in a room off the hall. Kennedy was tied to a rickety chair. He looked scared.

Jones kept his gun pointed at Frank as Adams pushed him into the room, sat him in a chair, and tied him up.

When Adams finished, Meyers turned to Kennedy. "Sorry it has to be this way, kid. All I wanted to do was make sure the festival didn't raise enough money. The robberies would have done the job if Frank and Joe Hardy hadn't decided to play hero. You can thank them for your dilemma."

"Turn him loose, Meyers," Frank said. "He's got nothing to do with your crazy plans."

"Turn him loose?" Meyers repeated with a snort. "No such luck, kids." Meyers stopped and looked around at what had once been a plush room. "Old Man Bradford would rather leave his money to a bunch of kids he never knew rather than to a Meyers. Well, this Meyers is going to have the last laugh."

"I'm curious," Frank said, stalling for time. "What made you wait until now to try to get the inheritance?"

Meyers smiled his yellow-toothed smile. "Good question, Frank. A detective right up until the very end. The truth is, I didn't even find out about Bradford until my grandmother died six months ago. When I was cleaning out her things, I found some old letters. She was Bradford's only child, and he didn't even leave her a dime. But that just means there's more for me. And nothing is going to stop me from leaving Bayport with what is rightfully mine."

"By 'nothing,' I take it you're not above staging a hit-and-run accident," Frank said. "Or framing Chet for the robberies."

"You deserve a star," Meyers said. "You've got it all figured out. Too bad it's not going to do you any good."

"My brother will be here any minute with the police," Frank said.

"Nice try, kid, but I happen to know better. The police have their hands full with the parade. And you know how I love a parade," he cracked. Turning to Adams and Jones, Meyers said, "I'm going to my apartment to get the money from the robberies. When I get back, we'll silence these two permanently."

"You'll never get away with it," Frank said.

Meyers laughed and turned toward the door. "I already have."

Joe screeched to a stop in front of the phone booth, jumped out, and dialed the police station. "I need to talk to Chief Collig right away," he told the officer who answered the phone.

"The chief isn't here," the officer said. "He's riding in the parade."

"Then let me talk to Officer Riley," Joe said.

"Sorry," the officer said. "Riley is out on the streets, coordinating crowd control."

Joe remembered seeing the floats lining up on Oak Street. If he hurried, he could find Chief Collig before the parade started. But that would mean losing sight of Frank and the white minivan. Joe hung up, spun around, and stopped short.

140

The van!

Joe searched the streets. The white van was gone!

Joe kicked the ground in frustration. Meyers had Frank, and now Meyers was gone. What should he do?

There was only one choice. Deciding to drive the streets, searching for Frank, Joe hopped in his van. If he couldn't find him in ten or fifteen minutes, then he'd head over to Oak Street and find Collig. He hoped by then it wouldn't be too late.

Over and over, Joe drove up and down the streets, but he couldn't find any sign of the white minivan. He must have looked at his watch a dozen times, worrying about where Frank might be . . . and what might be happening to him.

Finally, Joe decided he couldn't waste any more time looking for the van. He made a U-turn and headed toward Oak Street.

And then, just as Joe approached Oak Street, he spotted the white minivan going up the street. Joe made a sharp right and pursued the van.

At the next traffic light, Meyers stepped on the gas and squealed away from the intersection. He must have spotted me in his rearview mirror, Joe figured.

Joe stayed on Meyers's bumper as he drove up Oak Street. Soon they reached the floats lined up on one side of the street. Meyers had to drive up the street on the left side, since the parade was on the right, and Joe was forced to do the same. "I can't believe I'm doing this," Joe said to himself. "This is one time in my life I *wish* the police would pull me over. But there are none in sight. Where are they all when you need them?"

As Joe approached Park Avenue behind the van, he could see the police barriers blocking off the street. The parade would turn down Park Avenue and then head into the park. Meyers wasn't slowing down.

"Meyers, what do you think you're doing?" Joe yelled at the man through his windshield, though he knew he couldn't hear him. Meyers seemed to be following the parade route, and no one was trying to stop him. Finally Joe saw a police officer moving one of the barricades that blocked Park Avenue. Meyers sailed on through, and Joe followed him. The police must have seen that it was Meyers in the van and assumed he was performing his security duties.

"No time to stop now," Joe said as he briefly considered trying to explain the situation to the oblivious police officers. He was too close to finding Frank and Kennedy.

The sound of a marching band told Joe the parade had started. The lead float was only a few yards behind Joe. Meyers suddenly accelerated, and Joe had to step on it to keep up with him.

142

Meyers was trying to lose both Joe and the parade, but Joe had other ideas.

"Here we go!" Joe hollered.

Meyers went blazing through the park, with Joe right on his tail. The parade floats followed. Joe caught a glimpse of Chet's long black cape, his powdered wig, his bicorn hat, and his very surprised expression!

With Joe in pursuit, Meyers drove through the park, and they soon lost the parade. The white van reached the edge of the park grounds and turned into the Bradford estate. Now Joe knew exactly where Dan Meyers had been hiding David Kennedy.

Without hesitating, Joe whipped into the Bradford driveway and roared up the hill, pulling to a stop right behind the white minivan. Dan Meyers was heading into the mansion. Joe rushed inside after him.

"We have to stop meeting like this." Trevor Jones snarled as he jumped Joe from behind.

Joe braced his feet and rammed his elbow into Jones's stomach. Jones grunted in pain. Quick as lightning, Joe spun around and caught the man on the chin with a vicious uppercut.

"Behind you!" Frank yelled to Joe. Joe turned to see Frank, tied to a chair, across the room to his right. At the same moment, Adams took a roundhouse swing at Joe.

Instinctively, Joe dropped to the floor, sent Adams sprawling with a scissors kick, then caught him with a spinning back kick as the man tried to get to his feet again.

Jones, meanwhile, lunged toward Joe from the side. Joe put all his weight into his punch and hit him in the stomach. Jones gasped again and bent double.

"Get out of the way. I'll take care of him," Meyers said, appearing in the hallway.

"Watch out," Frank warned. "He's got a gun."

Joe dove to the side, sprang to his feet, and found himself looking straight down the barrel of Meyers's gun.

Meyers sneered. "He's all yours, boys."

Just then a loud commotion sounded out front.

Meyers glanced toward the door. It was the break Joe needed. He delivered a karate chop to Meyers's wrist, knocking the gun from his hand just as Chet—in cape and hat—rushed through the doorway. Craig Thompson was with him, along with Chief Collig and Con Riley.

Chet kicked the gun out of the way, tackled Adams, and with a swirl of his black cape, he sat on him. Thompson delivered three blows to Jones's head with his left hand, then a knockout punch with his right.

Chief Collig and Officer Riley rushed inside. Meyers lowered his head and charged at Joe, knocking him to the floor. Then he ran toward the back of the house. Joe heard the back door slam as he sprang to his feet. He bolted through the house and out the door.

Meyers was running through a stand of birch trees. He was twenty feet away when Joe turned on the afterburners. In a flying tackle, Joe took Meyers at the knees. They landed in a heap in a snowbank. After rolling around in the snow, Joe finally pinned Meyers by kneeling on his chest.

Chief Collig arrived seconds later, put the cuffs on Meyers, and took him back into the mansion. Joe stood up and brushed the snow out of his hair, watching as the chief disappeared inside the house. "Looks to me like Collig got the easy part," Joe murmured. Back inside, Joe found Adams and Jones sitting cuffed together on a sofa. Officer Riley stood guard.

Chet finished untying Frank and started working on the ropes holding Kennedy.

"I'm arresting you three for kidnapping," Chief Collig said.

"Don't forget the robberies," Frank said.

"We don't have any evidence linking them to the robberies," Chief Collig stated flatly.

"That's right," Jones said. "You can't pin anything on us."

Frank walked over, stood beside Officer Riley, and looked down at Adams and Jones. "So Meyers

145

has been playing you two for suckers," he said. "What was he going to do? Cut you in for a share of the robberies? That's peanuts considering that Meyers was going to rake in millions."

"Don't listen to him, boys," Meyers said. "He doesn't know what he's talking about."

"He doesn't, does he?" Joe asked. With that, he told Adams and Jones all about the trust. Their eyes widened when he got to the part about Meyers being the only Bradford heir.

Jones glared at Meyers. "Why, you dirty double-crosser—"

"Hey, that money is rightfully mine," Meyers growled.

"Meyers planned the robberies," Adams said, confessing now, while Dan glared at them both. "And when it looked like the festival was still raising cash, he decided to go after Kennedy. He had me fire the gun to spook the horse, hoping Kennedy would be injured. When that didn't work, he came up with the kidnapping."

"Did you throw the ax?" Frank asked.

"No," Adams said. "Jones did. We heard you telling your aunt you were going out to Jenkins's place. And when Meyers let us know that you'd be in the cross-country event, he had Jones cut the tree and push it over."

"How did you know we were going to be in the alley that time you ran us down?" Joe demanded.

"Meyers," Jones offered. "You told him you were going over there to investigate, remember?"

Joe realized that every step of the way, he and Frank had helped Meyers keep tabs on them. "So how'd you know we'd be out at the park late that night you threw Frank into the Dumpster?" Joe asked.

"That was just luck," Adams said. "We were tossing some more evidence into the Dumpster, hoping you'd find it and suspect Pender again. When we ran into Frank, we thought, why not rough him up a bit, scare him."

"They were in the perfect position to pull off this crime," Frank explained to the police officers. "With their security uniforms on, they could come and go as they needed to. That's how we lost one of them after he robbed the sweater booth. He ran to the alley behind the stores, and one of the shopkeepers let him in, assuming he was a security guard rather than a crook. No one thought to question them."

"And Meyers was in the perfect position to find out which booths were the best ones to rob," Joe added. "All he had to do was keep his eyes open for who was making the most money. And then his men swooped down on them."

"I've heard enough," Chief Collig said. "Take these crooks downtown and book them."

Joe turned to Craig Thompson, his hand extended. "I owe you one," he said.

147

Craig shook Joe's hand and smiled. "Believe me, I won't let you forget it for a minute."

"For a while, they thought it was you and Pender," Chet said.

Craig laughed. "I do odd jobs for Roger, but so far he hasn't asked me to rob anyone." Then he turned back to Joe. "Listen, man, I'm really sorry about the stunts I pulled. I loosened your blade just as a joke. I never thought you'd wipe out like that. I really didn't mean to hurt you. Let's call this a truce."

The younger Hardy ran a hand through his blond hair. He wasn't sure how much he trusted Craig's change of heart, but he might as well hope for the best. "It's a deal," Joe said.

Frank and Joe, with Chet, Craig, and David Kennedy, were left in the big old house after the police took the criminals away.

David Kennedy shook his head and said, "I never expected this much excitement in the little town of Bayport. I was planning on having a casual weekend with a couple of normal high-school guys."

Chet laughed and said, "Frank and Joe are anything but normal."

"Hey, what's that supposed to mean?" Frank said in mock anger.

David said, "I think I'll actually get more rest by sticking to my grueling workout routine. Seriously, how do you guys do it?"

"We just have a way of finding the action, I guess," Joe replied. "Don't forget, we got some help from Chet on this case."

"Chet, you came at the nick of time," David said. "How can I thank you?"

"Well, actually there is one thing. . . . Oh, never mind." Chet looked flustered.

"What is it, Chet?" David prodded.

"Oh, it's nothing. I was just wondering if—"

"You could have my autograph?" David guessed, looking amused.

Chet beamed. "I thought you'd never ask," he said.

The five boys stepped outside and saw that the lead float was pulled up next to the mansion. The rest of the parade, including floats, bands, and clowns, was strung out behind it. "I don't believe it," Frank said, and started laughing. "How did the entire parade end up here?"

Chet grinned. "When I saw the minivan go roaring by with Joe on his tail, I knew something was up, so I got my float driver to follow Joe," he said. "Since we were in the lead, I guess the rest of the parade stuck with us."

"Well, lead them back to town and get the parade under way," Chief Collig said. "The people of Bayport are waiting."

That evening exuberant fans packed the auditorium as Frank, Joe, and Chet made their way to

149

their seats. "Wow! The front row," Chet said, balancing two hot dogs and a cup of hot cider.

"The mayor said we earned them," Joe said.

"Ron Smithson was glad to get the stolen money back," Frank said. "The police found it in Meyers's apartment."

Just then the house lights dimmed, and music drifted from the loudspeakers. Thunderous applause greeted David Kennedy when he glided onto the ice. The spotlight followed him as he skated over to where the boys were seated. He shook Frank's hand, then Joe's.

"We all owe a big round of applause to Frank and Joe," David announced. "If it weren't for their great detective work, I wouldn't be here tonight." Frank and Joe grinned, and David went on. "And thanks to them, the festival raised over fifty thousand dollars for the hospital."

The crowd let loose with boisterous clapping and cheering, and David skated off, ready to perform his routine. As the skater began his first moves, Chet whispered to Frank and Joe, "Actually, they should all thank your aunt Gertrude. Wasn't it her great cookies that got us all involved in the first place?"

"If that's what you want to think, Chet," Joe said with a laugh, "go right ahead. I'm sure Aunt Gertrude won't mind one bit!"

R·L·STINE'S

GHOSTS of FEAR STREET®

THEY'LL HAUNT YOU FOREVER....

1 HIDE AND SHRIEK
52941-2/$3.50

2 WHO'S BEEN SLEEPING IN MY GRAVE?
52942-0/$3.50

3 THE ATTACK OF THE AQUA APES
52943-9/$3.99

4 NIGHTMARE IN 3-D
52944-7/$3.99

5 STAY AWAY FROM THE TREEHOUSE
52944-7/$3.99

6 EYE OF THE FORTUNETELLER
52946-3/$3.99

7 FRIGHT KNIGHT
52947-1/$3.99

Available from Minstrel® Books
Published by Pocket Books

POCKET
BOOKS

Simon & Schuster Mail Order Dept. BWB
200 Old Tappan Rd., Old Tappan, N.J. 07675

Please send me the books I have checked above. I am enclosing $_____(please add $0.75 to cover the postage and handling for each order. Please add appropriate sales tax). Send check or money order--no cash or C.O.D.'s please. Allow up to six weeks for delivery. For purchase over $10.00 you may use VISA: card number, expiration date and customer signature must be included.

Name _____

Address _____

City _____ State/Zip _____

VISA Card # _____ Exp.Date _____

Signature _____

1146-05